Jesse Leung

Metvan Stories

Depreciating Hope

Metvan Stories: Depreciating Hope by Jesse Leung

Published by Jesse Leung

Edited by Kristy Phillips

ISBN: 978-1-7782047-1-5 (ebook)

ISBN: 978-1-7782047-0-8 (paperback)

Created with Vellum

To Gautam, who was like a second father to me, helping me pick up the broken pieces of my life when I had hit rock bottom.

CONTENTS

CHAPTER 1

YOUTHFUL AMBITION

The hustle of Vancouver hummed softly by as snow lightly fell upon the seaport city. Once again, the residents, not accustomed to the snow, lumbered on their way to work, cursing the winter weather under their breath as they waited in long lines of stalled traffic.

Meanwhile, a twenty-one-year-old young man looked out the window from the fitness centre where he was training, smiling at the wintery scene. He'd been working out for seven months now and was the envy of other members—well-built and wearing a small shirt that emphasized his physique all the more. He'd been born with Lee as his last name, and his parents had named him Aaron. But he despised its traditional roots and preferred to be called Ron.

Leaving the gym, he walked over to his sporty blue muscle car and coincidentally looked over his right shoulder, seeing a young Asian woman reading a small novel by herself in her car. He'd seen her before, running on the treadmills, but he never had the guts to ask for her name or number.

Smiling mischievously, Ron got in and revved the car's

engine, creating a deafening roar to get the girl's attention and show off his ride.

Looking over at the wannabe hotshot, who had quickly donned a pair of snazzy sunglasses, she grinned but kept on reading her novel, not the least bit impressed.

Well, it was worth a shot, he thought.

He sighed and pulled out of the parking lot, merging into the main street, then headed for the university nearby. He had both economics and business classes throughout the week, and he desperately hoped that after graduate school, he'd get a decent job as a policymaker or manager of finance. His parents had always wanted him to attain an honourable and well-paying job so that they could boast to all their friends about just how great and accomplished their son was.

Realizing he might be late for his first class, he sped up to seventy kilometres per hour, still ten under the speed limit, but a white sedan on the opposite side of the street suddenly dashed for it. It made a hair-splitting turn left, causing Ron to immediately brake. The whiplash brought his head to within inches of the windshield, and he breathed heavily as the adrenaline and reaction to what just happened shocked him.

Blaring his horn in aggravation, he stuck his head out the window and yelled at the top of his lungs, "Watch where you're driving, idiot!"

But by then, the sedan had already driven off, leaving his angry shouts to dissipate into the silence.

Shaking his head in disbelief at the negligence of the driver, Ron made his way to the university's parking lot and picked the lot number 888—a number associated with wealth, luck, and prosperity in his family's culture.

Entering the classroom, he nodded apologetically to the professor for being late and sat down near the front.

Squirming to find the most comfortable position in the desk with its tiny chair, he settled for a half-slouched, half-stooped posture.

"Class, has anyone heard of the term *depreciation?*" the professor asked. "Today we'll be discussing its meaning. Essentially, it's a term used to define the deterioration, or decay, of capital over time. For as time goes on, most things break down, malfunction, or become faulty, just as humans become feeble the more years they have under their belt."

Twirling his pen, Ron imagined himself in a large woollen sweater, with a head full of grey hair and bent over holding on to a walker for support.

As Ron's mind wandered, the professor continued, "This decaying of human capital has inspired many explorers to find the proverbial fountain of youth—something that has eluded scientists even to this day. But according to legend, it was the search for a magical age-defying herb that led to Japan being colonized by two dozen Chinese youths sent by their emperor."

Chinese youths sent to find the magical herb, Ron thought. The words reminded him of the pretty Asian girl he'd seen outside the gym earlier. Her long eyelashes seemed to flutter every time she blinked, and her petite nose was nothing short of adorable. As the professor droned on and on in a monotonous tone, Ron hoped to have another opportunity to meet her and not act like a complete clown in front of her.

Taking the assignment handed out by the professor, Ron meticulously packed his stationary, papers, and textbooks into his knapsack before heading back to his car.

Driving to the badminton centre, Ron recalled when he first met Ben and Dave at the local badminton competition in Surrey several years earlier. In awe of Ron's victory in the final match, Dave and Ben had asked if he wanted to play some games with them at their local gym in Cloverdale. Ron had agreed to meet up with them, and the trio became a tight-knit group, practicing badminton every week without fail. Many times they bet on who would win, with the losers forced to drink a vile vegetable smoothy concoction that tasted just as bad as it sounded.

After he parked the car, Ron carried his badminton bag to the gym, along with a thermos of ice-cold water, which would have been perfect for a summer day.

"Hey, Ron! Did you see that match yesterday between Lee Dan and Lee Zhang? It was a-w-e awesome!" Ben said, as he walked along with Ron, each of them carrying their badminton bags to hold their expensive rackets. Ben was always one of the first to see the clashes of badminton titans around the world. His enthusiasm for badminton often needed to be grounded back to earth by either Dave or Ron.

Thinking back to the badminton titans from China in the past, Ben lamented at the lack of serious competition against the Chinese. "China's always got a hold on all the badminton tournaments. They even win most of the Sports Competition medals! What's their secret to winning all the time?"

As they approached the gym, their friend Dave caught up with them and joined in the conversation. "Don't worry," Dave said. "We've got a secret weapon ourselves—one of the best players in Vancouver. He'll be able to unseat the Chinese."

"Are you talking about me, Dave?" chimed in Ben with a grin.

"Very funny. No. We all know Ron's the best player of us all. He'll win it for Vancouver, for BC, for Canada."

Ron beamed with pride as he listened to his playmates compliment his skill, but he kept a modest attitude by complimenting his buddies' skills as well. "Hey, you guys aren't half bad too, you know," he said.

Starting their recreational matches, it was just as th players mentioned: Ron was the best among them, hitting smashes and drop shots, and sporting an impenetrable defence. In straight sets, Ron won game after game against his buddies, in both singles and doubles, showing that he was indeed extremely versatile in badminton. After several games in a row, most of Ron's opponents were exhausted, panting, and breathing heavily.

Ben commented between breathing gulps of air, "It's no use fighting a robot. Man! Ron, it's impossible to beat you!"

"Nothing's impossible, but hopefully it's enough to get me into the school team," Ron replied.

Patting Ron on the back, Ron's partner Stan reassured him of the confidence they had in him. "We do believe you can make the team, bud. It's just you who needs to believe it yourself."

Saying his goodbyes, Ron drove back to his parents' house in the suburbs of Cloverdale. Finally, back at home, he walked in the door and could smell his mother's wonderful cooking. The aroma of barbeque pork, fish sauce, and rice wafted into every corner of the house, making Ron extremely hungry.

"Dinner will be ready soon, Ron!" his mom called out.

"Thanks, Mom! You're the best. Smells like heaven!"

After dropping off his bags in his room, Ron plopped onto his bed and stared at the posters on his ceiling. Most of them were from superhero movies for children, but those were the ones he remembered and cherished the most, for they always had happy endings. He often daydreamed about whether his future would hold the same happy ending as depicted in those films.

Sitting down at the dinner table, the family began to eat. But as usual, his dad closed his eyes for a second before eating. Ron was surprised that Dad was taking this praying thing seriously. His dad had been changing slowly; no longer was he the happy-go-lucky man Ron had grown up knowing. Instead, he was more serious, knowledgeable, and strangely enough, content with his life.

It had all started about a year ago when Dad got sick with a high fever and chills, forcing him to be bedridden for several days. Frightened that he might not have much time left to live, he began digging around for something to save him, something to quell his fear of dying and becoming forgotten and nonexistent. For the majority of his life, Dad had focused on building up his company, Lifetime Supply Delivery, his pride and joy. The company had grown to a multimillion-dollar corporation specializing in endowment subscriptions and deliveries. After getting sick, he realized just how fragile life is, prone to be cruelly snuffed away by the slightest breeze. Mom, for the most part, tolerated his new beliefs, but she lost it whenever he tried to preach to her.

Ron chewed determinedly on a piece of pork, slightly annoyed and perplexed as to why his dad chose to be so strange—to be someone different. Ever since Dad's change, there had been many arguments between him and Ron, and there had been a particularly nasty one not two weeks earlier when his dad tried to preach to him.

"Ron, we aren't in control of our destiny. We were born to serve. Please, listen, my son. Look, if you want to kno—"

"I'd rather die than be a slave to anyone!" Ron had yelled at his father.

Bang!

Ron remembered how he had slammed his bedroom door shut in front of his dad. He had then gritted his teeth in anger, lying on his bed and struggling to banish any doubts he had about his atheistic beliefs.

Shaking away the memories, he busied himself with eating, trying his best to forget the feelings of annoyance when being preached at, and at the same time wondering if his dad would ever give up lecturing him.

CHAPTER 2

DISAPPOINTMENT

As if the change in Dad's behaviour wasn't bad enough, not two weeks later, Ron got some surprising and disappointing news. He and his buddies were in the lobby entrance to the university gym, waiting for news of recruitment for the school team. After what seemed to be an eternity, the head coach came out with an attempt at a comforting smile.

"Ron, I'm afraid that the standard for the badminton team is very high, and the skill level of our players is very professional. So I'm afraid you're not making the cut."

Ron scuffed his foot and looked at the ground, hiding his disappointment. "Thanks, Coach. Do I have to stay for the rest of the recruitment?" As the coach shook his head, Ron packed up his things and walked hurriedly out the doors, leaving his buddies trying to catch up to him.

A couple of days later, the gang met up again for their weekly games, but one person was missing. Ron didn't show up even nearly an hour past the time they usually started playing.

Ring, ring!

Ben was calling Ron for the fifth time. Having known Ron for years, he was worried by his absence from the court. Ben knew that Ron had high hopes and aspired to be a great Canadian badminton player, representing Canada on the world stage. Therefore, Ben knew failing to get on the team must have been especially hard on Ron's self-esteem.

Again, Ron didn't pick up, and Ben shook his head.

"Sorry guys, he's not answering. What should we do? I'm worried for him. It's not like him to be depressed like this. Dave? Stan? Any ideas?"

"He'll come around, just give him some time. I'm sure he'll be bounding back to play badminton with us sooner or later. We're his best buds."

Ben sighed as he put away his phone. "I just wonder if we should have put all those lofty goals in his head."

Dave shook his head. "I'm afraid the fine line between false hope and motivation is blurred. It's hard to tell how much to encourage and when to hold back. It would seem we over-motivated Ron."

"But Dave, we weren't being overly optimistic. Wasn't it the truth that we saw his potential to be a champion?" Ben's voice sounded with indignation.

"The problem is that the coach doesn't see it that way, although you do have a point there, Ben. I don't even remember winning a single match against Ron." Taking his racket, Dave joined the rest of the group starting their matches, but without their star player, Ron.

* * *

FAR AWAY FROM his concerned badminton buddies, Ron lay on his bed, pondering the future of his sporting career. He was at the point where discouragement had seeped into his inner being, corroding the confidence he once had in his sporting skills.

Ring, ring!

Ron looked over at his phone—Ben again. He knew they cared, but they couldn't see him in this state. He was devastated about not making the team, as his failure meant chastening the pride of his badminton buddies, the pride of his family, and the pride he had in himself. Failure had knocked him down a few pegs, and he would need to climb back up—if he had the motivation to do so.

Failure, that stubborn, idiotic word, he thought. He had worked so hard to avoid it, in school, sports, family, physique. Yet it somehow always devastatingly caught up with him. Punching his pillow as if failure had a face, he plopped back on the bed, sulking and grumbling about the unfairness of life and wallowing in his quagmire of self-pity.

Cocking an ear towards the washroom, Ron heard his dad singing:

"He is our refuge and strength,
An ever-present help in times of trouble.
If his love is measured in length,
Its end can't even be seen by the Hubble."

Rolling his eyes, Ron picked up his headphones and drowned out his dad's shower songs with heavy metal, hoping the next day would bring about better news.

Driving to school after a brief breakfast, he was in fact surprised when he got to class at Kensington Polytechnic University. Unfortunately, the news he got was not what he wanted. His final economic theory exam, worth over 30 percent of his final grade, got a mediocre result—a B minus.

Seeing his test mark, he cursed under his breath. This meant his GPA might fall below the minimum standard required for entering grad school at the best universities.

"Professor, do you have a moment?" he asked.

"Yes, Ron?"

"I believe we haven't covered this material in class, and I'm completely drawing a blank on how to answer these questions. I've checked all my notes and materials, and I've never come across these formulas."

"Those are questions designed to make you think, Ron. I previously mentioned in the test review class to look up formulas about the topic. And if you did as I asked, you would have known the answer to those questions."

"How can we be tested on something we don't know? What's the point in coming to class if we're just going to be tested on material we find on the web? Why do we even need you as a professor?"

"Ron, I don't appreciate being threatened. If you have a grievance, you may take it to the dean. Now, I must be heading off to my next class."

Frustrated, angry, and discouraged, Ron stormed off down the hallway with an emotionless face hiding the quivering sadness threatening to reveal itself. By the time he made it to his car, a single teardrop rolled down, and as he gripped his steering wheel in frustration, his anger was like a dam about to be breached. Lying back and shutting his eyes to the harsh sunlight, he remembered he'd promised his buddies he would start badminton again later that day. Deciding to rest a bit before going, he lay there, almost falling asleep in the warm afternoon. After driving to the gym, he was still

half-awake, daydreaming as the match started.

"Ron … Ron ... Ron! Wake up!" Dave said.

"Wha—" Ron looked up and saw Ben jump high towards the birdie and thunder down a smash that on any ordinary day would have been returned. But not that day.

"Sorry, Dave," Ron replied. "I'm … There's a lot on my mind right now."

"Can I pay you a penny for your thoughts? Is it about the school team?" Ben asked as he walked under the net and put his arm on Ron's shoulders.

"Ben's right, you're not yourself today. What's up, buddy?" Dave feinted several jabs at Ron, getting him to defend himself from the pretend barrage.

Walking over to the bleachers and sitting down, Ron explained to his buddies what had happened. "I bombed my final exam for economic theory, and with my new lower GPA, I'm not able to qualify for grad school at the universities I wanted to attend. I can't get anything more than a bachelor's, so my stupid dreams are out the window. It's just like badminton. I just can't reach my goals. I'm … I'm a failure."

Ben thought for a minute, then comforted Ron. "Hey man, you know, the word *failure* has an *l, i, a,* and *r,* and that spells *liar,* because no matter how good and successful you are, it would be a lie to say you've never experienced failure. No one escapes failure because it also spells *l, i, f, e, life.* Hence disappointments and failure are part of life. What is important is how you see failure. As a barrier to success or a footstool to help you reach higher next time?"

"Reach higher? What do you mean?" Ron asked.

"Just don't limit yourself. Try your best, and you'll be amazed at what you can achieve. It may not always be what you want, but you'll know that you gave it your all."

Hitting his racket on his knee as he absorbed what his buddies were telling him, Ron listened half-heartedly to their consoling advice. The more frustrated he got, the harder he hit his leg, letting the pain substitute for his frustration. Standing up from the bleachers, he started packing his rackets and bottles.

"Thanks, guys, for the pep talk. I just … I just need some time to think it over."

Ben and Dave watched as Ron walked with a slight limp in his left leg, out the propped-open doors, until he was out of sight. Both of them hoped that their friend would bounce back, but they had a flicker of suspicion that Ron would spiral into depression if he couldn't find his life worth living.

CHAPTER 3

RESPITE

As he parked his sports car at the gym, Ron felt like he was carrying the heavy burden of failure and discouragement. He sat there contemplating whether or not he should even try to work out. He shut his eyes for a brief moment, pausing to organize his thoughts.

Knock, knock!

Opening his left eye Ron looked out the window and saw the girl he had revved his engine at before! Bolting up, he accidentally knocked his coffee mug and spilt his decaf all over his clothes.

"Oh no! I'm terribly sorry. I didn't mean to scare you. Honest." The girl looked apologetically at Ron, turning red with embarrassment.

Ron opened the car door and shook off as much coffee as he could from his clothes. "Don't worry about it. Now I can bless people with caffeine alertness by just walking by them. One sniff and they'll have their buzz."

The girl grinned at his antics in trying to make her feel better. She pointed her mitten-covered hands at the gym. "Are you going to work out at the gym again?"

Ron nodded. "I was just getting ready to go in until the, uh, coffee. It's been a rough couple of weeks, so I'm not quite sure where my head's at." He held out his hand to introduce himself. "The name's Ron, and your name is?"

"Penelope, or Penny for short. It's nice to finally meet you. You're not the first one to rev your engine at me." Penny rolled her eyes and started laughing as she saw how embarrassed Ron was. "Don't worry about it. I usually just ignore cool guys who act stupid. So I'm sorry I didn't say hi. So you just going in to work out?"

"Yeah, I usually got my regimen for each workout session. Today's my arm day."

Both Ron and Penny stood there, embarrassed and blushing red as a pair of roses. Walking in together, laughing at odd jokes and chatting, they both went on with their training regimen. Ron opted for bench presses while Penny chose to do crunches then balance with the yoga ball.

Ron couldn't help but gaze at her, admiring her slender, fit body and beautiful, long jet-black hair. As she caught him staring, Ron immediately turned away, embarrassed and trying hard to seem focused on his weightlifting.

Looking at them both, one would have never guessed they were strangers. Both were smiling and laughing as if they had known each other for years. Indeed, it had been a while since Ron had had such a huge smile or laughed as hard.

After giving Penny his number, Ron wiped the beads of sweat off his head with a towel and watched as she drove off. On his way back home, he couldn't help but reminisce about his encounter with Penny. She was such a sweet, gentle girl—and someone who listened to him, hearing him out on his troubles, joys, and problems. He could have talked with her all afternoon. It had been one of the best days of his life by far.

As he walked into the house, Ron's mom looked up from her cooking, signalling his dad to their son's late arrival.

"You're a bit late, Son," his dad said. "Any later, and we would have eaten dinner without you. Were you busy?"

"Sorry, Dad. Something awesome came up at the gym."

Dad looked at his son and instantly recognized Ron was in a good mood. Smiling at Mom, he interrogated his son. "Alright, Son, what happened? You're chirpier than a bird, and I haven't seen you smile like that in ages! Good news, I hope? Come now, don't keep me guessing!"

Looking at his parents, Ron realized just how infectious his smile had become, as both were beaming at his sudden change in mood. Ron smiled all the greater as he sat down. "I met a girl at the gym. Her name's Penny."

"Yep, honey, it's a girl! I knew it!" his dad crowed. "What's she like? I thought I recognized that expression. It was just like me when I first met your mom."

"Yes, dear, you had the goofiest grin on your face as you sat down with me for coffee," Ron's mom said. "If you smiled any longer, you would've developed a permanent clown face." She shook her head in laughter.

"Silly as it was, she still went on a date with me!" Ron's dad said.

"And I haven't the foggiest idea what came over me to do such a thing."

"Oh, honey you're too kind." Dad reached over and kissed Mom on the cheek, which she promptly wiped off. But she smiled back.

"Penny and I have a lot in common. We both believe in protein shakes, low-carb diets, and cleansing detox drinks, not to mention she likes badminton as well!"

"Tsk tsk, it takes a health junkie to appreciate another health junkie," Dad said with a chuckle.

"You could do with some healthy routines too, honey." Mom patted his growing gut.

"Your cooking is far too good to pass over, dear. See? My belly is a compliment to your amazing culinary skills!" Turning to Mom, Dad winked at her affectionately.

Mom's cooking was indeed one of the best, and that night's dinner was no exception: roast beef, gravy, mashed potatoes, and cheesy Brussels sprouts.

A week later, Ron flopped onto his bed and looked over the selfie pictures he had taken with Penny at the gym over the past few days. Her smile was so calming and delightful, and they deeply enjoyed the time spent together. They had gone to the mall for their first date, ordering ice cream bars coated with peanuts and white chocolate. Walking together along the brightly lit hallway, Penny held on to Ron's hand as they strolled past the shops side by side. Stopping at a jewelry store, Ron pointed to an engagement ring and raised an eyebrow, as if wondering what Penny thought of it.

Laughing out loud, Penny simply dismissed the idea, chiding him for being so rash. "Slow down, bud. We've only been dating for a week!"

After taking a few selfies in front of a beautiful water fountain, they tossed several pennies into the water, making secret wishes in their minds.

Not to say the least, Penny's skills at badminton were exceptional. Ron introduced her to his buddies and started to play mixed doubles with her on his team. Penny covered the net surprisingly well, while he covered the back and handled any clears. Pretty soon, both of them were synchronized as a team, knowing where the other would go and where to cover. Their teamwork was like clockwork, as if they were meant to play together as fate would have it.

One day when they were playing together, Penny blocked another flat shot, scoring a point. Ron praised her and encouraged her to keep it up. "You're on fire, Penny! Awesome block! Careful, the right side."

Finishing off the last match without conceding more than ten points, they left the court to get changed. As Ron went to the change room, Ben and Dave took Penny aside and chatted with her.

"Thank you so much, Penny, I've never seen Ron so happy in his life!" Ben said. "Especially since his disqualification from the most prestigious grad schools. I honestly think that's the first time I've heard him laugh so much for almost a month."

"Ben's right. He's no longer thinking about his failures when he's thinking about you," Dave told her. "But if you do get the chance, Penny, help him learn not to feel depressed when life throws a wrench into his plans."

Giving them a thumbs-up, she looked up and saw Ron walking towards them.

"Hey, Penny, I'm done. Let's head to the theatre?" Ron said.

Ben and Dave watched them go, both grateful to see their old buddy back.

CHAPTER 4

THE ROARING YEAR

After coming back from the gym, Ron eagerly changed and then gulped down some water as if he were facing a ten-year drought.

"You're looking chipper today. Off to see Penny again?" Dad smiled and winked at his son.

"Yeah, we're off to see the new movie, *Maladie de la tête.* The reviews for it were pretty good, so it should be rad."

"What's its rating?" asked Dad as he raised an eyebrow.

"Don't worry, Dad. It's rated PG. I'm not a kid anymore. Besides, they're only movies. It's not real."

"I'm not worried about whether it's real or not, I'm worried about the content—you know I don't approve of explicit or crude films. Trust me, once you open that rabbit hole of obscenity, it's a long, long rabbit hole down. And the further you go, the harder it is to get back up."

"How would I know, Dad? Ever since I was a kid you've never let me watch a single explicit film. How can I know if it's good or bad for me?"

Dad's eyes fell in embarrassment and his tone grew more solemn. "Trust me, Son. I've … I made the same mistake when I was your age. There's not a single week that I don't regret ever taking that route in life. Don't make the same ill-fated mistake as I did. What I do, I do to protect you. You'll see later on. You'll understand."

Ron stood in the doorway looking quizzically at his dad. There was a part of him that wanted to trust his father and listen to his advice, but another part of him resented his father, despising his newfound moral values and resisting his ever-growing constraints.

Who gave Dad the authority to control what I can or cannot do? Ron wondered. *It is my life and my choice. I'm the commander of my own ship. I should be the one to take charge of my own destiny.*

Grumbling to himself about his father's rules, he got in his sports car, pulled out of their home's driveway, and headed off towards the movie theatre. Parking a good stone's throw away from the entrance, he got out and checked the time: seven o'clock. He was fifteen minutes early.

Leaning on the side of the wall outside the entrance, he resumed one of his pastimes: checking his phone for new social media posts among his friends. Scrolling through the updates, he noticed a new post by Penny talking about a boy she was dating. Reading more, Ron smiled as he realized the post was about him. He made a mental note to write a post as well about Penny.

Looking up, he saw Penny coming, wearing an ugly Christmas sweater. He waved at her calmly, but inside he was happy and eager to see her.

"You should have told me to wear an ugly sweater like yours!" he said, laughing.

"You look better in those extra-small T-shirts of yours. An ugly sweater doesn't suit you." Penny patted his back. "You look good, my boy, trust me."

Holding the door for Penny like a true gentleman, Ron

gestured towards the snack counter, where the smell of melted butter proved almost irresistible.

"Do you want popcorn?" he asked. "I'm sure they have a non-fat,

non-GMO, and vegan variety. What do you think?"

Penny laughed. "No, it's okay. I'll just take some water. Did you want one too?"

"Sure, but here, let me pay for it."

"You're a real gentleman, Ron" Penny smiled at his slight embarrassment.

"And you're a proper lady. But one who can't cook." Ron smiled back mischievously.

"Come on! I only burned the salad once—maybe twice."

Ron tutted at her. "Should we remember the food poisoning you gave me with the undercooked chicken or the time you cut your finger?"

"Fine, fine, you're right. But I'll try my best to learn to cook one day. I'm getting tired of eating arugula salads and avocado sandwiches."

Pulling a disgusted face, Ron remembered how, when Penny invited him to visit her parents for the first time, he was extremely nervous about making a good first impression. Unfortunately, he had made the wrong decision to stay for dinner, as Penny's family often ate healthy but bland food, like salads, veggie sandwiches, and low-sodium soups. Ron had tried his best to gulp down the dinner, but a part of his stomach wanted to heave out all the healthy rubbish. Penny felt bad for Ron as she watched him down mouthful after mouthful of green puréed soup, and she nervously laughed as he tried to keep up a smile.

Penny's parents kept a sharp eye on Ron, questioning him about his future prospects in life. "So, Ron, are you in school or are you working?" her dad asked.

"I'm currently finishing up my undergraduate degree in

economics and business, and I'm hoping to get into graduate school for a master's degree."

Piping in to help Ron's image look better in front of her parents, Penny told her parents about some of Ron's achievements and skills. "Ron is a very good badminton player and has won several small tournaments in and around Vancouver. He can also bench press a hundred and fifty pounds!"

Nodding, Penny's parents smiled approvingly at Ron, whose ears turned slightly pink as Penny boasted about his accolades.

Ron came crashing back to the present as they entered the auditorium. The two of them silently watched the movie, engulfed by the emotional plot and intrigued by the emphasis on a person's mental well-being. By the end, Ron and Penny were thinking deeply, both pitying the movie's character, who was suffering from a mental illness, and feeling sad that no one was there to save him from his depression except his wife, who was on the verge of leaving him. When the man gained control over his delusions, Ron and Penny were relieved and happy that the couple would be able to move on with their lives. The ending, while still tragic, had an element of hope that gave it an optimistic feeling.

While the credits rolled, Ron sat there thinking, astonished at how much the main character's life resembled his own during the early, disappointing years before he met Penny. Both he and Ron had fallen into depression and needed much time to recover and retry at life.

"Hello? Earth to Ron, Earth to Ron." Penny's voice transported his thoughts back to reality.

"Yes, yes, Penny, you were quite right, quite right."

Standing up, Penny put her hands on her hips and shook her head. "I didn't even ask anything! She laughed. What were you so deep in thought about?"

"I just was thinking how that guy's life resembled my life. My struggles, my problems. It just struck me how identical that story was."

"Then perhaps you'll reach the same happy ending, bud. Who knows? It could be possible. You've got to be optimistic, Ron."

"Too bad life doesn't usually have rosy, utopian endings such as this one. The real world is dark, grim, brutal, and, most annoyingly, unfair."

Penny shook her finger, indicating he was mistaken. "That's where you're wrong, my boy. Life is fair, but it depends on if you see life with contentment or with resentment. It's a choice. Will you be content with what you get or will you resent what you have?"

Ron smiled back at his girlfriend. "Oh, you are so wise, Madame Penny. Thank you for gracing us with your wisdom."

Penny swatted at him in mock anger. "Call me madame again, and I'll make sure never to bake another cheesecake for you."

Putting on a face of mock horror, Ron instantly repented, dodging her swinging arms. "Oh, Miss Penny, beautiful Miss Penny, my apologies for the offence. Please forgive my rude address—Ooof!"

Ron reeled as one of her swinging arms connected. Faking an injury, he fell over as if mortally wounded.

Penny couldn't stop laughing at his theatrics. "You're the worst performer, Ron. I barely grazed you with my hand!"

"Yes, but such a graze from such a beautiful woman can be romantically fatal."

"Ron, you're like a lovesick puppy." She laughed again. "Okay," she said. "Let's keep walking. The credits are rolling."

When they reached the exit, Ron kissed her goodbye,

then they walked to their cars. Ron was putting on his seat belt when Penny went roaring past his car.

Honk! Honk!

As she drove by, she had a mischievous grin on her face. Then she waved farewell.

Ron smiled and waved back. She was a fantastic girl—he couldn't have asked for a better girlfriend.

Listening to the radio as he drove back home, the uplifting country music had him singing along as he sped through 64th Avenue in Surrey back towards Cloverdale.

Pulling into the driveway, Ron paused, smelling the air freshener that Penny gave to him and recalling when she first entered his ride.

"Your car smells like sweaty socks with a hint of beer" he remembered her saying. She'd made the most horrid face when she opened the door. After appearing to make several vomiting chokes, she ran away, covering her mouth. Then the very next day she gave him five or six individual air fresheners smelling of citrus, which became an aromatic reminder of her.

As Ron entered the house, Dad looked up from his newspaper. "So, how did things go?"

"Everything went well. We both enjoyed the movie. I think it's about time we shared our relationship status on social media. You think?"

"Just remember, if this blows up, you'll probably regret making a public announcement. Son, you have to be careful what you say on social media—once you put it out there, you can't take it back. Ever."

"Uh huh. I think I know what you mean, Dad. So, what did you and Mom do when there wasn't anything like social media? Did you announce your relationship by word of mouth?"

"Oh, simple really. We just held hands wherever we went. With the occasional kiss, of course."

Ron fidgeted as he recalled his rude address to his dad earlier. "Dad, I'm sorry if I acted rashly before heading for the movie. It's just, I appreciate having you as my dad, but I want to figure out the important things by myself. Does that make sense?"

Giving Ron a thumbs-up, Dad replied back straightforwardly. "Ron, I likewise should apologize if I was too pushy trying to get you and your mom to see things my way. But if you're ever in doubt, I'd be glad to help the best I can. If you want, that is."

Walking to his room, Ron took out a strip of small photos from a photo booth in the South Surrey Mall. Peeling them off, he stuck them onto his wallet, smiling at the goofy faces he and Penny had made for the photos. It had been nearly half a year since they first met over the spilt-coffee incident. She was gentle and kind, and—best of all—she understood him at a level deeper than even his closest friends or family comprehended. She was an exceptional listener, and that was the perfect matching trait for Ron, who needed someone to share his burdens of disappointments and frequent depression.

Standing up, Ron grimaced as a slight pain in his side flared up. Going into to the washroom, he splashed water on his face and thought nothing of the pain, as if it were not a big deal. Returning to his bed, he lay there with pleasant dreams of enjoying life with Penny and his future family dominating his thoughts. As the minutes turned to hours, his eyes drooped lower and lower until he was deep in slumber.

CHAPTER 5

ACCIDENT

"Penny! Cover me!"

Diving to return a drop shot at the front of the net, Ron couldn't stop fast enough and careened into the metal pole holding the net up. He was feeling woozy, as if he was drunk, so Penny helped him get to the bench. He sat down, rubbing the growing lump on the side of his head.

"Anyone got ice?" Penny called out. "He's hit his head pretty bad. Ron! Can you say something? Ron?"

Blinking several times, Ron stood back up and smiled, wanting to continue the match that had been abruptly interrupted. "Thanks, guys, I'm fine. Lost a few brain cells though probably." He laughed weakly.

Looking at the benches around him, Ron suddenly noticed Ben's bag had switched colours, from green and blue to red and orange. Thinking nothing of it, he dismissed it as a figment of his imagination and went right back to the match with Penny.

Penny helped him back up, laughing at the lump on his head. "Now I can call you Egghead, eh?"

Rolling his eyes skyward, Ron refocused on the game,

blinking twice, as he could have sworn Penny had been wearing a headband just a few moments before. Playing his best and having the most fun he'd had since he was a carefree child, Ron smiled to himself. Life was finally giving him a break that he so desperately needed.

As Ron drove back home from the recreation centre, he thought the trip seemed quicker than normal despite the flow of traffic typical of a late evening on a weekday.

He took a shower before crashing onto his bed, then he called Penny to say goodnight. He guessed she would be working on her studies, with midterms coming up.

"Hey, Ron, what's up, bud?" she replied. "I'm just about to wrap up my kinesiology studying and head off to bed."

Ron laughed, as he had predicted correctly. "If you do that, you'll be dreaming of yoga balls and physiotherapy equipment."

"Hmm, might be a good thing. Would help me remember all those procedures for my test tomorrow."

"Well, just wanted to check up on you. Wish you a good night. Sans bedbugs."

Hearing Penny chuckling on her side of the phone, Ron said one final goodbye before crawling into bed himself, wishing the weekend would come sooner so he could have more time with Penny. They had agreed to go to a laser tag arena on Saturday, and possibly another movie on Sunday night as well.

* * *

WHEN HE SHOWED Penny his graduation certificate as evidence that he had achieved his Bachelor of Arts degree, Penny pretended to rip the piece of paper, to Ron's horror. Realizing that she was only joking, he shook his head in disapproval, snatched his award back, and put it safely inside its protective folder.

"One day you're going to give me a heart attack, always scaring me like that!" he said.

"A little fright never hurt anyone. Keeps you on your toes too."

"I'm going to need to keep an eye on you, little mischief-maker!"

"Oh Ron, you've always had an eye on me, staring that is!" Penny laughed. "Ever since we met at the gym! What were you thinking about while looking at me?"

"Oh, um, you know. I thought of kissing you, of us holding each other ..." Ron put on a nervous smile, clearly embarrassed at the nature of the question.

Patting his back, Penny laughed, admitting she too had entertained such thoughts. "I thought of that stuff too, Ron. Don't worry, it's not just you. It's mutual affection. Though I doubt there'd be someone who wouldn't love a pretty little package like myself."

Dropping his jaw at the egotistic comment, Ron shook his head when he realized she was only playing with him.

"Gotcha there again, bud!" Penny said with a big laugh.

Grabbing her with a bear-like hug, Ron planted multiple kisses on her head and face as if chastising her for her prideful remark.

All joking aside, they had a small kiss before getting into the car and driving to the laser tag arena. They lined up at the registration desk, with Ron paying the entry fee for them both.

Gearing up in the equipment room, they decided to be on the same team, working together as a unit covering one another. After a brief demonstration of how to shoot and other rules of the game, they heard the door open, and adrenaline immediately rushed through their bodies as they ran for the nearest cover.

Aiming at the back of one of the opponents, Penny scored several shots before shooing Ron to move back to avoid being detected. Rounding a turn, they suddenly found themselves faced with another opponent. Ron quickly shot him multiple times in the front before running for cover with Penny.

Cheering out loud as they were declared the winners, Ron and Penny headed back to the equipment room to start the next game.

Once all the games were over, they took off the vests and headed to their car, just as a slight drizzle of rain began to fall.

After driving Penny back to her house, Ron gave her a kiss on the cheek and dropped her off, waving goodbye before heading back to his home.

Walking through the front door, he found his parents huddled around the aquarium, with worried looks on their faces.

"Hey Dad, Mom. What's up? Something wrong?"

Shaking his head, Dad relayed the bad news concerning one of his fish. "The oldest catfish isn't doing so well. He's not eating, and he's swimming awkwardly near the surface."

Pointing at the poor animal, Dad let out a loud sigh, knowing this would happen sooner or later. "He was more than five years old. A very long lifespan for any tropical fish. If he doesn't improve by tomorrow, I might have to flush him to end his misery."

Putting a hand on Dad's shoulder, Ron consoled him as best he could, but he knew that the fish meant much to his dad, who had raised and cared for various generations of fish since his childhood.

CHAPTER 6

TRAGEDY

"Hurry, Penny, he's in critical condition. It may be our last time to see him. His appendix ruptured, and it's not looking good." Ron's mother sounded extremely nervous on the phone as she relayed as much info as she could to Penny.

Throwing aside her homework, Penny rushed to her red sedan, putting on the Bluetooth connection to her phone. "I'm on my way to the hospital. Please tell him to hold on."

It was only three weeks till Christmas, and even the thought of not having Ron around for the holidays was unbearable for Penny.

Weaving throughout traffic, Penny was coming towards the intersection leading to the university Ron had attended when suddenly a pickup truck turned left, cutting in front of her. She was unable to stop fast enough. Her sedan crashed into the truck and her windows cracked into a thousand pieces, shattered beyond repair.

"Penny? Penny? What's wrong?" Ron's mom almost shouted into the phone. She cast a worried look at his dad and started walking away from Ron's hospital bed.

"Mom? What's wrong with Penny?" Ron said weakly as he looked over at Mom after waking up and hearing Penny's name. He was going into emergency surgery in a few minutes and had hoped to see Penny just in case it was the end.

His mother stepped back inside and reassured Ron that everything was alright. "Don't worry, Ron, it's nothing. She's probably just busy. You need to rest, Son. You'll get better soon, and we'll all be together again."

The reality was, they would never be all together again. Penny suffered critical injuries and was soon fighting to stay alive in the ICU. The following day she succumbed to her injuries, and the doctors were unable to revive her.

A few days after the surgery that miraculously saved his life, Ron wondered why Penny hadn't visited him. "I don't get it, Mom, Penny's not responding to my texts or calls. I'm worried for her."

Dad looked with a sad face towards Mom, shaking his head as if to tell her not to reveal what had happened to Penny. He then relayed to Ron what the doctor had said earlier in private to Mom and himself. "There is some bad news. The doctor said you'll need to stay in the hospital for a few weeks to treat the infection that developed in your body when your appendix ruptured. But your surgery is finished, so you'll only get better from here onward, Son. Sans appendix."

Ron took the remote and turned on the TV, which was broadcasting the news.

The anchor was saying, "On Monday night, a crash in Surrey's 128th Street—"

Bleep! His mom took the control out of his hand and promptly turned off the television.

"Hey, Mom. I was watching that!"

Putting the remote in a drawer on the opposite side of the

room, Ron's mother smiled. "Doctor's orders are to rest, Son. Don't bother with the TV. Just focus on getting better, alright?"

"That's fine, Mom. Penny will bring me up to speed on the current news when I see her. She is coming, isn't she? Sometimes I feel the only reason I'm alive and getting better is because of her," said Ron as he looked out the hospital window.

Smiling the best they could without seeming suspicious, Ron's parents waited till he dozed off before conversing quietly.

Mom had a worried face, wondering if keeping the truth from Ron was such a good idea.

Several hours later, a hospital worker approached the family and introduced himself. "Mr. Lee, Ron? Hi, I'm your physiotherapist, Jared. I'm going to help you for the next couple of weeks to keep training your muscles instead of lying in bed all day. I hear you used to be a badminton player? So, let's try to get you back on the court by Christmas. How's that?"

Hearing the optimistic suggestion, Ron cracked a smile, hopeful that he would be back to normal in no time. "Thanks, Jared, I'd like that very much."

"First, let's work on sitting up. We're going to let you try to sit up all by yourself with no assistance from us."

Ron shifted to a better position and easily pushed himself up with his elbows, but not without a twinge of pain in his abdomen.

"That's very good, Ron. Let's practice sitting down and sitting up a couple more times today, okay?"

Within two weeks Ron was sitting up and walking without much pain, but he still required a wheelchair to get around.

"Take it slow, Son!" his dad said. "Slow and steady wins—"

"The race. Yes, yes. I know, Dad. I feel like that kid in the movie who learns to run without his braces. Run, Ron, Run!"

On his final week, he was lifting a small dumbbell while in his chair, counting twenty repetitions before looking at his parents, feeling accomplished. "Dad, Mom! I did it! Oh, I can't wait to show Penny!"

"You did excellent, Ron," his dad cheered. "You should be well pleased with your progress, though I must warn you to not overdo it."

"Oh, my boy is getting better, thank goodness!" exclaimed Mom as she held back tears.

"It will feel so good to hit the gym again and play badminton with Penny." Ron said. "Will Penny be there when I get back, Dad? I haven't seen her in nearly three weeks. It's not like her to ghost me like that."

"Let's take things one thing at a time, okay Son?" Dad dismissed Mom's worried face as she looked his way. "Everything will be alright in the end."

After signing all the necessary paperwork to be discharged from the hospital, they got into the family SUV and drove back home.

As they pulled up to the house, Ron felt emotional seeing his sports car there, as he dearly missed driving his sleek blue ride. "Does my sports car still run?" he asked. "Did you guys keep it maintained?"

Dad nodded, assuring him that they looked after his car with utmost care. "Yes, Ron, we made sure it would be in picture-perfect shape for your return."

Sitting in his wheelchair and pushing himself beside his car, Ron glided his hand over his car's exterior frame, then rolled in the front door with a push from his dad.

He insisted on walking up the stairs to his room and, with Dad and Mom supporting him, made it to his room door. Inside were mountains of get-well cards, gifts, and presents that had accumulated over the nearly month-long hospital stay. Searching amongst the gifts, Ron kept looking for anything from Penny, but disappointingly, there was nothing from her.

"Mom, you said that Penny was busy? Why didn't she send any gifts or write anything to me?"

Mom looked from her son's hurt expression to Dad's stern but sorrowful gesture not to worry Ron about Penny.

"She just couldn't get you anything, but don't take it seriously," his dad said. "It's not her fault. She just can't." His serious tone left Ron even more confused, but he decided that at least Penny would be pleased with his progress.

A few days after returning home, Ron wanted to get back into badminton. So he phoned up his buddies, talking through the speaker phone. "Hey Ben, Dave, it's been ages since I saw you guys. I got the video message you sent to me at the hospital. I'm happy I have such good friends like you guys; you've always got my back."

"It's great you're doing so well, Ron, but we won't go easy on you in badminton!"

"I'd want it no other way, boys! Losers buy drinks again? I'm afraid no beer this time, but how about floats or smoothies?"

"Sounds like a deal, Ron. You're on!"

True to their word, the boys didn't go easy on Ron, winning 21-2, 21-3 and a shocking 21-0 for the third and final game.

By the end, Ron was sweating and panting, but he seemed to grow stronger with each passing day. He also started training at the gym again, hoping to see Penny somehow at the same place where he had met her. He even visited her parents' house on several occasions, but they wouldn't tell him where Penny went. Day after day, his hopes of seeing her were dashed, as there was no sight of her anywhere.

Starting his training again was extremely difficult. Before his surgery, he could bench press over a hundred and fifty pounds easily, but now he had to start from scratch, struggling to lift just the bar. Slowly but steadily, he was getting fit again, strengthening his weakened muscles and building up endurance.

He asked the office staff at the gym and found out that Penny hadn't been to the gym to work out for more than a month and that her account had been deleted for unpaid membership. He tried asking Ben, Stan, and Dave where she went, but each time he asked, they wouldn't answer him no matter how much he pressured them.

After another visit to Penny's home to no avail, he drove back home. He took in deep breaths smelling the air freshener— his best memory of Penny now that she was gone.

But something didn't seem right to him. After knowing him for over a year, why would she suddenly ignore him for so long when he needed her most? Looking at the air freshener, he saw that it was almost finished. He made a mental note to buy more of the same fragrance.

Arriving back home, he took out his phone, and he scrolled to the last post Penny made about him.

I am so lucky to have Ron in my life,
I've been with him during the best of times, as well as the worst.
I can't imagine my life without him,
Please keep him in your thoughts.

He just couldn't understand. How could Penny write so affectionately about him one moment and suddenly cut off all communication, leaving him when he needed her most? Scrolling through the countless selfies of them both, he hoped that fairly soon they would be together again.

He remembered how contagious her laughter was and

how hard he had tried to make her happy even on her worst of days. There was something in him, some inner voice, that kept telling him Penny would never give up on him. But that just made him even more confused as to where she had gone.

One morning after more than a month back from the hospital, Ron woke up in time for breakfast. He walked downstairs to find Dad, as usual, reading the paper. Dad looked up at him over his glasses and cracked a small grin. Ron was slowly coming back to normal.

Ron had weighed just a hundred and thirty pounds only one month before, but now he was a healthy hundred and sixty pounds. His face no longer was gaunt as it had been when he was in the hospital.

"Penny wasn't at the gym again," Ron said, his tone of voice dropping off as he stared at the floor, clearly demoralized.

"Son, I know you miss her. I can't say I blame you. But you need to centre your life on something more important—"

Bang!

Ron had barely listened a bit before running and slamming the door on his father's help. Dad sighed heavily, walked upstairs to his son's room, and gently knocked.

"Go away. I don't want your preaching," Ron called out.

"Son, I'm not gonna preach. I want to tell you what happened to Penny—"

Before he could finish the sentence, Ron yanked open the door and looked eagerly at his father's face.

"Ron. She's gone for good."

"What do you mean? She left and moved somewhere else?"

"No, no. She got in a car accident the day you had your surgery."

Ron's hands fell limply to his side—the news hitting him

like a punch to the gut. "Did ... Did she survive?" His voice was now trembling and tears were just about to start streaming down.

"She passed away a day after the crash. I'm sorry, Ron."

Speechless, Ron walked backward slowly until he sat down on his bed, too shocked to react to what his dad just said to him. Quivering, he held his hand over his mouth, disbelief drawn all over his face.

"No, no! This can't be. Why didn't you bloody well tell me sooner?" Tears of sadness turned to tears of rage as Ron glared at his dad.

"We all wanted you to recover physically and mentally before we told you the truth about Penny. It was for your own good, Son"

"Get out!"

Walking out, Dad looked back as his son glared at him. "Sorry, Ron," he said. Turning back around, he slowly pulled the door shut and sighed deeply. Waiting just outside Ron's room, he could hear the sobs from the other side of the door, saddened that he'd had to break the news to his grief-stricken son. Looking briefly at Mom, who had peeked up the stairway curiously, he wondered if keeping Penny's death a secret had been such a good idea after all.

He and Ron's mom walked back to the kitchen, then they both went about their business, letting their son mourn over his loss.

A couple of hard and depressing weeks later, Ron started bouncing back, but he was not the same person he'd been before, even as he returned to his usual hobbies.

"Mine! Cover me!" Ben shouted as he and Ron were playing doubles. The previously weak, feeble Ron was now nearly as strong as he'd been before the surgery. Ron jumped up and hit a thundering smash, sending the birdie streaming into the opposing court.

Taking a break, everyone sat on the bleachers, and there was an uncomfortable silence among the friends.

"Ron, you're playing angry. That's not good for you, you know? Sport shouldn't be an outlet for your emotions, bud. It takes the fun out of it." Ben's voice sounded like a wise man giving advice.

"Why so serious, Ron?" chirped Dave.

Giving an annoyed eye to Dave for yet another jesting remark as everyone else laughed, Ron looked down once again, scuffing his feet.

The laughter of the group died down and everyone patted Ron's back, giving a little comfort to try to fill the enormous hole in his life. No one dared mention her name, but it was apparent her absence and Ron's emotional toll were definitely related.

CHAPTER 7

CLIMBING OUT

A physical geographic depression is a pit, and likewise, Ron's depression saw him wallowing in the bottom of the pit, not even trying to get out. Learning of Penny's death was a serious blow to his motivation, joy, and contentment.

Taking out his wallet, he touched each miniature photo of them together. It was one of the only ways he could look back and remember her.

One day he parked his sports car at the gym and, out of the corner of his eye, thought he saw Penny, sitting in her car on the phone. Excited in disbelief he rushed to open the car door—only to see the memory fade away, leaving no trace of its existence and just an empty parking spot.

Setting up the bench press, Ron trained intensely, if only to momentarily forget the tragic loss in his life. Pushing himself harder and harder, he refocused on exercise to keep his mind busy, which helped him avoid the deep and painful memories of losing Penny.

As he walked outside, the cold winter air blasted against his face. He shut his eyes, letting the warmth leave his body and cool him down. The discomfort of the sheer cold reminded him of the hard times that had befallen him—the losses, the sadness, and the gross unfairness, in his opinion.

Catching a snowflake in his hand, he watched as the beautiful, delicate crystalline structure melted away into an ugly droplet of water. The snowflake was gone forever. Never to return.

Driving along the road to the badminton centre, Ron was approaching where he'd heard Penny had crashed, just outside the university. He momentarily thought he glimpsed her crawling out of the mangled vehicle, hurt and bleeding. But just as quickly as it appeared, the vision vanished, leaving Ron all the more confused.

Back in the badminton gym, he stretched his legs and, for the third time that day, saw Penny. This time she was playing a game on the court.

Walking up to her, he reached out his hand. But once he touched Penny's hand, she disappeared into the thin air. It was just another memory—a façade of reality seared on his brokenhearted brain. She was right about him all along: he was like a heartsick puppy.

Starting the game, Ron served, saying, "Love all." He focused on the badminton, once again escaping to the ideal land of preoccupation—distracting himself from the truth. But it was impossible to forget the synergy, teamwork, and cooperation he had experienced playing with Penny as his partner.

"Service over, twenty, game point, eighteen," Ron called out as he was about to win the match against Dave. Ron's retraining and recovery had indeed been good, and his badminton skills were also reviving. His friends, though, noticed he seemed distracted, as if he was thinking of something other than the game itself.

For no matter how hard he tried to forget, he didn't—and

perhaps couldn't—stop thinking of what life would have been like with her.

Changing to their regular clothes, they chatted about recent events and things they had heard about the past week. "Yo, Ron. I heard you got into grad school," Dave said. "Are you going back to get a higher degree?"

"Yeah, Dave, I got accepted at the business school grad program at Stikine University—at the Vancouver campus. It'll be weird trying to get used to studying again. You can't teach an old dog new tricks, you know."

"Ron, you're not even thirty! You're not considered old. At least not yet, bud."

"Well, I feel old. I don't have the energy I used to have. I can barely get out of bed on time, let alone play badminton for three hours. Pretty soon they'll need to use a cattle prod to get me out of bed."

Stan dismissed his feeble grumbling with a matter-of-fact response. "It's a miracle you can still play badminton, so stop your whining."

"Yeah, Ron. Would you like some cheese with that whine?"

Ron rolled his eyes again, not even amused at Dave's corny joke. But afterward, Ron cracked a smile, grateful for his dear friends.

Leaving the gym, he wondered what being a student once again would feel like, as it had been more than two years since he'd studied for his undergraduate degree.

Before starting his schooling again, Ron had to get the necessary supplies that were key to succeeding in school, or so he believed. Walking through the office supply shop with Mom, Ron started picking out his stationery and supplies for returning to school.

When he picked a D-ring binder with a pull-tab for easy

opening, his mom gasped at the price. "Ron! That binder alone is twelve dollars! Is it really worth it?"

"Good education begins with good stationery. And don't fret, Mom. I'm paying for it myself." Picking a few brand-name ballpoint pens and mechanical pencils, as well as quality erasers, Ron brought it all to the cashier to pay for it.

Walking out of the store, Ron asked his mom, "So what do you think of me going back to grad school? Think it's a good idea?"

Mom turned and looked affectionately at her son. "Of course it's a good idea. You were a good student. And when you finish, you can find a good-paying job so your poor old parents can boast to everyone about how wonderful their son is."

"Yes, of course, be the best for the pride of my parents," Ron said with a laugh.

"That's the truth! We do have the best son ever."

"Oh Mom, you're so humble"

"Ron, just finish grad school and prove we're right."

After unloading the stationary into his room, Ron watched his mom start cooking in the kitchen. After skill-fully dicing the carrots, zucchini, and cabbage, she turned to cutting the barbeque duck and removing the skin to be eaten separately. The simmering broth emitted a delicious aroma that made Ron's mouth water.

Looking out the window, he saw his dad mowing the lawn using the cordless electric mower. For some reason, Dad struggled with the cordless mower just as badly as he had with the corded one.

Ron opened the sliding door and shouted over the hum of the engine. "Dad! Do you need help? Dad! Dad!" Waving his hands, he tried to flag down his dad to see if he needed help.

His father finally noticed, cocked an ear, and removed his earmuffs. "Something you need, Ron?"

Ron slowed down his speech to make it easier for his dad to understand over the mower. "Do. You. Need. Help. Mowing?" He pronounced each word emphatically and with a great expression that even a novice lipreader could understand.

Shaking his head and waving his hand back towards the house, Dad signalled that he was fine.

Ron smiled as the mower ran away from his dad for a second. He even burst out laughing as his dad chased the mower halfway across the lawn. The runaway mower made a diagonal gash that ruined the perfect lines in the manicured grass.

Smelling the roast duck, bone marrow broth with noodles, and stir-fry vegetables, Ron helped set up for lunch and waited for Dad to come back from the yard work.

Everyone was exceptionally proud of Mom's cooking, and she beamed at the compliments thrown at her.

"Absolutely delicious, Mom!" Ron said.

"Dear," his dad said, "you've done it again. Such a wonderful meal. I wonder if any other woman could cook as well as you, my dear. You're the best!"

Dad laughed but noticed his son looking downward after the remark.

"I'm sorry, Son, I didn't want to remind you of Penny."

Wiping away a tear, Ron shuddered. "No, it's okay. I just remembered how Penny couldn't even make a proper salad." Shaking off the sad feelings, he continued eating, smiling to try to hide his unconcealable emotions.

Casting glances at one another, Mom and Dad both got up and rushed over. They hugged their son and regretted peeling open the wound that just never seemed to heal. It was a wound that ever continued to bleed their son's heart of the joys and contentment of life.

After dinner, Ron lay on his bed looking yet again at his

superhero movie posters taped on the ceiling. He kept wishing he'd been a hero who could have saved Penny from that car crash. If only he could have frozen the oncoming truck, shot a line of webbing to pull her to safety, thrown a grappling hook to pull the car back—anything to save her.

Turning his head towards his desk, he looked at the air freshener he had recently bought. He picked it up and opened it to let the pleasant aroma waft all over and fill the room with the familiar scent. As he lay there smelling the fragrance, his pleasant thoughts of Penny took a horrific turn and transformed into a frightening nightmare.

"Ron! Help me! Help me, Ron! I need your help, Ron! Don't leave me!"

Ron's forehead beaded with sweat and he sat upright like a bolt, looking back and forth at his room.

Penny! Where are you, Penny? he thought. In his mind, she had just been there, but he eventually understood it was just a dream. Lying back down, he was reminded once again that he hadn't been there to save her, that he hadn't been able to do anything to prevent her crash, that he'd been unable to protect her. He was reminded that this nightmare was real, and there was no waking up from it, ever. Hurt and feeling alone, Ron cried throughout the night, his tears staining the pillow where his head lay, whimpering, sobbing and unable to sleep, fearing that yet another gut-wrenching nightmare would appear.

Smelling the delicious aroma of hazelnut-flavoured coffee brewing, Ron woke up with dried tears encrusted on his face. He went into the washroom and washed them off with water. He looked at himself in the mirror and tried some self-motivation. He had to be strong, hopeful, and resilient. He had to move on somehow, someway, somewhere. But he understood that Penny would always be remembered in a part of his mind.

Yawning as he followed his nose downstairs, he couldn't wait to dig into Mom's cooking, which never failed to impress.

"Finally waking up, sleepyhead?" his mom said as she put a generous portion of omelet and some toast on his plate.

"I'm up, I'm up, but kinda tired," he told her. Taking the chocolate hazelnut spread, he began spreading it on the buttery toast.

"Here's some coffee as well. It's nice and hot," she said.

Sipping the coffee, Ron savoured the slightly acidic taste with a rich, dark flavour complemented by the aroma of hazelnut. "Is there a hazelnut theme today?" he asked. "Hazelnut coffee and hazelnut spread?"

"You don't like hazelnuts?" Mom tsked him. "Ron, why are you eating your toast with a knife and fork? Use your hands, dear."

"I have OCD, Mom! I don't know what kind of germs are crawling all over my hands—"

But after taking a dramatic pause, he dropped the cutlery and picked up the toast with his hands, smiling at his panic-stricken mother. "Gotcha there, Mom, didn't I?" he said. Ron smiled mischievously as he tapped his mom's shoulder.

"You scared me half to death, Ron," she replied.

"So, how's your schooling coming along? I assume you've been studying every night in your room."

"I've got a couple of midterms coming up, but I think I'll ace them. You were right, Mom; I am a good student." He laughed.

"Oh? Who's the humble one now?" Mom winked at her son.

"It must run in the family." Ron winked back at her.

Pulling up at the gym for a midweek exercise session, Ron went back to training, making sure to balance his exercise with schoolwork and sports. He now weighed nearly a hundred and eighty-five pounds, most of which was pure muscle.

But before starting the weightlifting, he opted to warm up with cardio, running on the treadmill for about half an hour.

While he ran with an incline, the TV in front of the machine constantly bombarded him with news, political scandals, and the latest gossip.

He then benched nearly his full weight and deadlifted a hundred and fifty pounds. He performed nearly twenty-five reps every set and at least ten sets per exercise. By the end of the session, Ron was drenched in sweat as he wiped down the equipment with an antibacterial wipe. He never really understood why people were so preoccupied with killing germs. He believed that immunity came after being exposed to germs and letting the body identify and eradicate them. Nevertheless, he followed the rules and decided that being considerate was more important in this case.

Next, he started work on his core, repeating crunches hundreds of times before being satisfied with the amount of training he'd done for his midriff.

Using the fifty-pound dumbbells, Ron worked on bicep curls until his arms felt like they were going to fall off, but he spurred himself on, driven by the desire to get stronger.

The last workout was for his legs, utilizing a leg press and putting on one hundred pounds as a counterweight. By the end of the exercise, every part of his body was aching, but the feeling of finishing something, of accomplishing a full workout, felt good to him. Some part of him was just glad that he was doing something useful and not wallowing in his slough of pity.

Moreover, his success in working out was the sole reason people commented to his parents about how good their son looked. Tall, muscular, and handsome, many daughters were introduced to him by parents trying to arrange a marriage with the well-built boy.

But these attempts would prove futile. The girls Ron was introduced to never met the Penny-like expectations he had for a future wife. Penny had been the perfect partner, and looking for another to fill her shoes was near impossible.

School was also a success for Ron, as he fit right into the academic lifestyle. With his hard work, tenacity, and resilience, he averaged As in his graduate courses and was on track to finish his master's degree in another year.

While writing a final exam on yet another business course, he came across an economic concept that had been introduced to him in his undergraduate years—depreciation. The concept brought him back to the lecture where he'd first learned about it and dismissed it as not relevant to a youth like himself who had everything going for him.

He shook his head at the naïve, carefree attitude he'd had back then and wished that he had been more appreciative of the time he had in his prime. He now understood why human capital also depreciated. People grow old; babies become toddlers; toddlers become children; children become youths; youths become adults; adults become parents; and parents become grandparents. He now knew that this progression, or anything similar, to it was inevitable. How he wished he was a youth again and not an adult already. But then again, he looked forward to and imagined what parenthood would be like. It seemed like something he would enjoy greatly.

CHAPTER 8

FLYING HIGH

Reading the invitation to try out for the Canadian badminton team, Ron and his buddies contemplated if he should give professional badminton a shot.

"They say second chances don't come very often, Ron," said Ben as he patted Ron on the back.

"But failing twice will also hurt twice as much. Honestly, you guys really think I should apply for the Canadian team?" Ron asked.

Stan conveyed what everyone else was thinking. "You're the best badminton player I know of in Vancouver. You need to try to make the team. Ron, it doesn't hurt to try if you give it your best."

"Well then, Ben and Dave, you guys should be my training group. What should we practice today?"

Dave tried to think of what Ron could possibly need to work on, as he was a good all-rounded player. "Your smashes are pretty good, but let's work on overhead clears, alright?"

The team changed into court clothes and began feeding shuttles to Ron, who would clear them overhead to the opposite end of the court.

"Aim for the third line, Ron! All the way back. A weak clear is like asking for a smash." Dave shouted his advice while motivating Ron at the same time.

Soon the entire court was littered with shuttlecocks haphazardly strewn all over the floor. Ron was sweating profusely as they neared the end of their training, having almost continuously trained for more than an hour. They started picking up shuttles and packing them back into their cases, excited but somewhat nervous about the recruitment later that week.

After the training session, the rest of the week flew by as Ron prepared for his tryouts at the Richmond Dome. Shuttles were also strewn about at the recruitment centre, but picking up shuttles wasn't a concern for the recruits, as workers at the centre took care of the cleaning. Ron was tested in his drops, clears, smashes, and defence, and despite being slightly older than the average recruit, he passed the tests with flying colours.

"Mom! Dad! I've got good news! I got accepted to the Canadian national badminton team!" Ron was practically leaping with excitement as he held the acceptance letter.

"I'm so proud of you, Son!" his dad said. "Congratulations! We're both proud of you! Are you going to be competing in singles or doubles games?"

Ron's huge grin subsided a bit. "It's just singles, Dad. Every time I play doubles, I think of her. She'd always be on my mind. You know, she was the best badminton partner anyone could ask for. So yeah, I'm just sticking with singles."

"I think this calls for a celebration! I'll order pizza for dinner." Mom smiled as her son's eyes lit up. "I thought that might brighten your evening. I'll call you when the pizza arrives."

Ron walked up to his room and quietly closed the door. Opening his laptop, along with several large textbooks, he began working on a project for his business course. Making a pie chart on the privatization of businesses in Vancouver, he noticed the pie chart looked like a pizza.

He smiled. It had been a while since the family had pizza. Hearing Mom ordering it was like hearing a cat bark—something even rarer than a blue moon. Having the health expert Mom in the family meant almost all meals were relatively healthy, but at the cost of flavour. Butter was never used, animal fat was limited, and a variety of vegetables, along with rice, made up most of the meals, with meat being served only in moderate portions. Furthermore, Dad had stopped eating pork lately, so pizza made it tricky to comply with everyone's tastes.

Catching himself in his daydreaming about food, Ron resumed working on designing a presentation on PowerPoint, adding text and informative graphics, along with charts, animations, and linked videos. He had made many presentations as an undergrad, so he knew how to captivate an audience and how to earn points from his professors.

Reading out loud the material to check for errors, he also made sure to reference all images, quotes, and facts. Using encyclopedias only for images, Ron made sure never to use them for proofs of information as quotes or textual references, as professors disapproved of encyclopedias. To use one would have been academically fatal for his grades.

"Ron. Pizza's here. Hurry before we eat it all." Ron could barely hear Mom, as she was a quiet, gentle woman who didn't raise her voice except in an emergency—or in the rare case of a heated argument with Dad.

Leaping and bounding down the stairs, Ron could smell the delicious aroma wafting from the large cardboard boxes filled with one of his favourite foods.

Dad had his cheese pizza, but Mom and Ron shared a

Hawaiian and pepperoni pizza—enough to feed a small army.

Picking up a slice, Ron watched the gooey cheese stretch like a string, and he comically tried to drip the string into his mouth, slightly missing and getting cheese on his face.

Dad laughed at his son's antics. "Ron, you're eating like a six-year-old. Use a napkin, boy!"

"His shirt is eating more cheese than his mouth is." Mom shook her head in disbelief.

"No other way to eat pizza," Ron said. "Messiness is just part of the meal. Leave me be!" He laughed as he picked cheese off his shirt. He ate the escapees as well because he remembered his mom's rule to never waste food. She had told him many times that children in Africa were starving to death, so he shouldn't waste anything. Ron used to believe examples like those when he was younger, but now that he was nearly twenty-four, he had come to believe and realize that things like wasting food weren't as important as Mom had made them out to be.

To be honest, Ron believed he knew much more than his parents. He had been the first in his immediate family to finish university as an undergraduate, and pretty soon he'd be the first to finish grad school as well.

With all this knowledge, Ron dismissed most of his mom's truths to be old wives' tales, and he was suspicious of his dad's truths as well. School had taught him to trust in science and empiricism. He'd learned to look to the facts and believe what those facts revealed.

Dad had given him a book that tried to prove his religion was real from a scientific perspective. Ron read the whole book and was still unconvinced because none of the book's points were substantial enough to prove they were real. Relying on patches and fragments of old texts, accounts of eyewitnesses, and other quasi-proofs, the book's lack of solid evidence made Ron even more skeptical.

But he had to admit there was something very different in his dad's character. He seemed to know something but could never explain how he knew it—saying only that there was no problem too tough for him to help with. Throughout all his struggles in the previous few years, Dad had always been there to support him and offer guidance.

Ron thought back to the countless times he'd slammed the door in his father's face as he tried preaching to him. Yet Dad never gave up, day after day and week after week.

Looking at his father, preoccupied with his cheese pizza, Ron noticed several white hairs on the side of his head, and in his beard as well.

A small voice in his head repeated a long-stored memory in Ron's brain: *human capital depreciation.*

CHAPTER 9

SUCCESS

For the next few months, Ron worked hard at his studies, and now, the final grades for his last four courses were to be revealed online at nine that morning, sharp. His mom had yet again offered to buy pizza if he had enough credits to earn his coveted master's degree in business.

Indeed, it had been a little less than a year since they'd had pizza together as a family, which Ron once again attributed to Mom's health-conscious mindset. He made a note to himself that once he moved out of his parents' house, he'd be sure to be a frequent visitor to the pizza parlours.

As Ron paced around the computer with his dad sitting in front of the screen, they both waited for his grades to be revealed, making a note that Mom's pizza offer was conditional upon successfully graduating. But as he waited, Ron suddenly froze and made a note—a mental note. The air freshener! He'd forgotten to buy more of the air fresheners that Penny had given him more than two years before.

"Keep refreshing that screen, Dad, the grades should come up soon," Ron said as he bolted for the door.

"Son where are you going—" But Ron had already left, and Dad sighed, looking back at the computer. "Sometimes that son of mine … He just reacts. He needs to slow down. He must've gotten that from your side of the family, dear."

"What was that, honey?" Mom poked her head into the dining room.

"Oh, uh, I'm perfectly fine, sitting here happily," he said.

Mom had the utmost confused look and went back to her cooking, muttering something to herself about husbands and potatoes. "Duds and spuds," she said.

Pressing the refresh key once every three seconds, Dad had the exciting task of finding out his son's grades the moment they were submitted.

Meanwhile, Ron was at the hardware store looking for Penny's air freshener, but it was a task much harder than he had expected.

As he walked down the fragrance aisle, every whiff of cologne, perfume, air freshener and spritz was in stock, overwhelming Ron's nose so much that he felt like he was suffocating.

He wondered how he was going to know which air freshener was the right one without smelling each one by one. Taking each freshener individually and trying his best to smell its unique fragrance, it took about fifteen minutes for him to find it. The freshener smelled of citrus, cinnamon, and mint and had a bright-blue liquid that seemed to resemble window-washing fluid.

Holding his precious cargo, he returned to his car and removed a flyer stuck to his windshield wipers.

Badminton Tournament @ the Surrey Sports Gym
10:00AM – 6:00PM

A smile crept across his face. If he had the time, he just

might give it a try. He could put the prize money away for a new car—not that he didn't like his blue sports car, but he thought that a new, sleek, dark-grey pickup truck would be rad.

Ron recalled the moment the keys to the muscle car had been handed to him at dealer after he'd convinced his dad to buy the car for him. This sense of responsibility and maturity washed over his emotions. He had chosen blue because it reminded him of the clear-blue skies and pristine blue oceans around the world. The car represented his coming of age, no longer needing Mom or Dad to chauffeur him to his destinations. He was taking life into his own hands.

Plugging his phone into the car, he made a hands-free call to his dad's phone to inquire about the grades.

"Nope, nothing yet," his dad said. "We'll let you know when they do come out."

"Should I pre-order the pizza?" Ron asked.

"Careful, don't count your chickens before they hatch. We should wait until the grades are submitted and have confirmation that you got your degree. By the way, your mom is betting that you'll get straight As in all four of your classes. If she wins, I have to give her a big kiss. And clean the bathrooms."

Ron laughed, thinking of his dad cleaning the toilets, vanities, and showers, scrubbing away at the soap scum. He remembered hearing about how Dad had worked for a fitness company for three months cleaning the stalls, showers, equipment, windows, and carpets in the wee hours of the morning.

That was before he ultimately became an entrepreneur, starting a subscription delivery service, which he managed from home. He recently had a newfound hobby of writing philosophical papers along with novels, taking inspiration from his past experiences, which Ron found rather unexciting. For all he knew, his dad had grown up just like everyone else he knew, living a cookie-cutter life, getting married, having kids, and doing what everyone else did generations after generations before.

Back home, Ron brought his fresheners in. As he walked up the stairs, he missed the look of acknowledgement on Dad's face as he glanced at Ron's mom, signalling to her about the air fresheners.

Once their son was out of hearing range, Dad quietly spoke. "He's been buying those air fresheners for his room and car ever since, well, ever since he met her."

"I keep thinking that he's moved on and going forward. But every time someone or something reminds him of her, he sinks back into his depression," Mom said.

Dad held up a finger to his mouth, motioning to talk softly, as he knew Ron was sometimes listening and would be worried if he found out they were fretting over him.

"It will take time to heal, and he is healing. I mean, he's back into badminton with his buddies and he's doing good in school," Dad said. "But he's not the same, and I don't think we should expect that. I do think he's doing the best he can to move on. We just have to be sensitive to whether he's down or not, because when he's down, we'll have to pull him back up. Otherwise, we may hurt him even more by being insensitive."

Mom nodded in approval, stirring her soup with her ladle. Dad was right, they would need to be more attuned to their son's feelings.

Ron lay in his room, breathing in the aroma of the air freshener. Several textbooks lay exposed to the harsh light of his desk lamp with floating motes of dust wafting around.

When was the last time I dusted my room? he wondered. *Gah, a little dust never hurt anyone.*

Holding on to the air freshener, he looked closely at it and noticed the logo of the company that sold it: K.T. Penny.

With a fresh wave of tears coming down, he now understood why Penny had picked that particular air freshener—it would remind him of her. He held the freshener to his chest, feeling all the unfairness and cruelty the world had to offer.

Then, as if on cue, Penny's lecture to him on fairness resurfaced: "Life is fair, but it depends on if you see life with contentment or with resentment. It's a choice. Will you be content with what you get or will you resent what you have?"

He could still remember her voice telling him to keep going, to stay motivated, to never give up.

Take it one step at a time, he thought.

Searching his mind, Ron decided to take Penny's advice from over two and a half years earlier. He decided to start with the baby step of thinking first about what he was content with presently.

Starting with the obvious, he was thankful for food and his friends, as well as the care from his parents. But beyond that, he was stumped as to how to continue. He could hear Penny's voice explaining again how to be content.

"We tend to focus more on what we want, thinking we'll be happier with rather than without. But in reality, we already have much to be happy about. It's just our human nature to grumble and want more and more."

Trying his best not to be depressed for Penny's sake, Ron concluded that even though he couldn't be with Penny anymore, he was thankful for all the time they'd had together. He would treasure it forever, however short it had been.

"Ron! Come quick!"

Hearing his dad shouting, Ron quickly wiped away his tears and bounded down the stairs—almost colliding with Mom as he stormed into the dining room.

"What? What is it?" he cried out. As Ron tried to look past his dad to see the computer screen, Dad broke the news in a trembling, excited voice.

"Looks like you passed all your courses, bud! You finished your degree! Congratulations, my boy!"

Struggling to contain his excitement, Ron covered his mouth, unable to conceal how happy he was that he finally had finished his graduate studies.

The feelings of accomplishment, relief, and joy after all his hard work in academia mixed together in a jumbled bag of emotions. The degree was worth it in the end. He remembered the struggles, especially in the beginning when he was adapting again to academic life.

Now that his schooling was finished, he could finally look forward to finding a job, something that he had eagerly awaited ever since he started his degree.

Checking the registry online, Ron had indeed earned straight As in all four classes of his final semester, meaning his father lost the bet he had with Mother.

Smiling gleefully, Mom laughed and rubbed in the fact that she won. "Dear, looks like you owe me a kiss and a clean-up of the washroom."

"Here you go honey," he said. *Pfffffffftttt!* Dad blew a big raspberry on Mom's cheek, and she yelped in surprise. Half laughing and half yelling at her childish husband, she swatted him away.

Picking up a roll of paper towels, a sponge, and cleaning powder, Dad set off towards the washroom, getting to work on the two full-sized washrooms in the house.

Dad hadn't liked the liquid cleaners ever since aerosol spray from cleaning products nearly suffocated him while he was cleaning a tub. Sticking with the powder cleaners, he'd learned from his mistakes and left the door to the shower tub open. Washing the outside of the toilet bowl, he gasped at the splash marks on the side of the vanity and on the underside of the seat.

It had been over thirty years, as Dad claimed, since he'd started urinating sitting down after his mother complained of splashes and inaccurate streaming. By the time he married Mom, his habit of sitting down was already well established and spared her the mess, most of the time.

Looking at the summary of his grades, Ron noticed that his GPA was roughly 4.00, which equated to an A in every course on average.

That would look pretty good on my resume, he thought. He just hoped that it would lead to a job that would be worth it —preferably in the field of business and finance.

Meanwhile, Mom called the pizzeria for the second time in nearly a year, and Ron eagerly waited to indulge in the greasy, cheesy goodness. He knew it was against every fibre of Mom's being to order nonhealthy food, but given the occasion, she was willing to celebrate together with the family.

Ten minutes later, three large pizzas filled the dining room table: Mom's favourite Hawaiian, four-cheese for Dad, and vegetarian for Ron.

As Dad was washing up to prepare for the pizza brunch, Mom handed Ron a knife and fork, which made him smile.

"I'm not a baby, Mom, who eats pizza with a knife and fork?"

"You will always be my little baby. Just use the cutlery."

Ron rolled his eyes, took the utensils, and started sawing away at the crust. As Dad sat down on his side of the table, Mom handed him cutlery as well. He complained in mock horror: "I have to use them as well? I'll take it, but under dissent, you hear?"

Putting on his saddest face that would melt a heart of ice,

his antics were unsuccessful, as Mom stood, unwavering in her decision.

"You both are going to use cutlery like good, decent human beings. I don't want to hear any excuses from either of you!"

Grabbing a slice of her Hawaiian pizza with her bare hands, Mom ate with gusto, much to the horror of Ron and his dad, who immediately protested.

Mom took one look at them both and said confidently, "I paid for the pizza. I get to decide who uses cutlery and who can use their hands."

Ron's and Dad's jaws dropped so low in disbelief that they almost touched the floor.

They looked at each other and burst out laughing at the hypocritical dictatorship of their mother and wife.

A little later, Ron put all the leftover pizza in a consolidated box and helped Mom clear the table. Then they put the leftovers into the fridge.

"Wow, Dad. You ate seven slices? Where does it all go?"

Mom winked at Ron and said, "Garbage in, garbage out."

Ron screwed up his face in disgust. "Gross, Mom!"

Ron thought that perhaps Mom's health-conscious disapproval of pizza as garbage still predominated in her mind, but it was nice she allowed it this time.

To his mom, health was of primary importance, and happiness for her was associated with being physically healthy and strong. Ron grew up holding on to the principle of good health as a means of contentment; yet now that he was older, he'd began to realize he could be happy while sick or likewise unhappy while healthy.

Pulling out his newspaper, Dad continued his daily routine of reading the ads for deals and sales at the local department stores.

"Honey dear, do you think we need a new vanity for

Ron's bathroom?" his dad said. "I noticed the sealant was black with mold when I cleaned it this morning. We could try resealing it again with caulking, or we could replace the whole thing."

"I wouldn't mind a new sink," Ron said, sticking his head into the dining room after eavesdropping on their conversation.

"Easy for you to say, don't you think? We're the ones paying for it!" said Mom as she wagged a finger at her son.

Tapping his head as if thinking, Ron agreed. "Why should I pay? Isn't it a parent's responsibility?"

"What an ungrateful little dog! We should have let you pay the bill for the pizza then!" said Mom as she folded her arms.

Ron gasped in mock horror as his parents smiled mischievously, threatening to make him pay out of his pocket. "Oh, merciful mother and compassionate father, you wouldn't force your only son to pay for his pizza, would you?"

"Your acting is pretty horrible, Ron," his mom said, laughing.

"Your mother's right," Dad added. "You shouldn't give up your future job for acting. You'd starve before making it on the stage"

"Well, humph. Thanks for both your votes of confidence in me. Honestly though, I've taken several drama classes. I'm not that bad at acting, am I?" Ron asked.

"To be not bad is, let us say, a long shot for you. Just do what you're good at doing and leave the acting to your aging parents," Mom said. Then she swooned, pretending to faint.

Dad caught her in the nick of time, letting her fall nearly to the floor as her hair grazed the ground.

"Mon amour," Dad said, staring into her eyes, which were

blinking ferociously, flirting with her husband as if they were still teenagers.

Ron hid his face in a book, smiling but somewhat embarrassed at his parents' antics. Under the cover of his textbook, he left the romantic pair and sneaked upstairs to his room to escape the drama that would've put any soap opera cast to shame.

Once again, he breathed in the aroma of the freshener in his room, which acted as a soothing agent for his thoughts, clearing his mind and helping him remember the joys of the past.

As he closed his eyes, patterns began to dance in his mind's eye and slumber slowly took over Ron's thoughts.

I now pronounce you husband and wife. You may kiss the bride.

There was Penny, dressed in white and looking as radiant as sunlight. Her long dark hair seemed to flow over her gown. Gently lifting her veil, Ron moved closer to kiss her when suddenly everything turned dark and he spiralled back into reality.

Waking up, he rubbed his eyes, erasing the scene of the wedding chapel and returning to the monotony of his room.

Cramming his eyes shut, he tried as hard as he could to bring back the wedding, to bring back Penny, but blackness was all he saw, swallowing up his imagination into a wormhole of nothingness.

Unable to recollect his dream of Penny, Ron walked groggily towards the sink. As the ice-cold water hit his face, reality snapped firmly into place, ultimately dissipating any trace of his dream like a waft of smoke.

Smelling the delicious scent of bacon on the stove and hearing the sizzling of eggs frying, he hurried to brush his teeth and wash up before leaping down the stairs for breakfast.

"Whoa, ouch!" Half sliding, half falling, Ron tumbled

down the stairs like a bowling ball but managed to land on his feet.

"How many times did I tell you not to run down the stairs?" Mom glanced unapprovingly at her seemingly stubborn son.

"Correction, I wasn't running, I was falling down the stairs." His nervous smile tried to stand against Mom's glaring judgement, but it melted down into an apology as his cheeky excuse was not the least bit entertained by her.

Sitting down at the table, Mom served the Ron and his dad a humongous portion of scrambled eggs and buttery warm toast with peanut butter spread. There was salty bacon for herself and Ron.

Devouring strips of bacon, Ron looked up at Dad and said, "Don't you ever miss eating pork? I'd rather give my left kidney than forgo eating bacon or sausage."

With a hint of a long-distant desire in his eyes, Dad calmly responded, "Bacon breakfast sandwiches were one of my favourite morning meals. Three strips of bacon, cheese, and buttery buns—it's delicious! I also do miss Chinese sausage, or *lap chung*, barbecue pork, and *sui mai* dumplings. But after nearly seven years, I'm fine without them. Not to mention, I'm now healthier than I've ever been in all my years."

With a dreamy look still on his face, he cut an egg in half, let the yolk run out, and used his toast to sponge up the liquidy ooze.

Shrugging off Dad's reasons, Ron attacked his plate with gusto while adding a spoonful of sugar to his coffee.

Mom tsked him. "Are you drinking syrup? That's a ton of sugar, dear!"

"Life's not sweet enough, so I compensate with my coffee," he replied.

Dad rolled his eyes at the corny joke. "Don't look at me, honey. I didn't teach him that line."

Meanwhile, Ron kept rolling with the puns. "Would you be a sweetie, Mom, and hand me the toast?"

Furrowing her eyebrows, Mom handed him the toast with a fair warning that if he continued with the jokes, she would impose consequences.

"Don't you two think of me as a sweetheart?" Ron asked.

Both parents rushed to stop the flow of horrible jokes, chasing Ron back to his room with his coffee.

"Sweet dreams!" yelled Ron before shutting the door.

Mom and Dad were laughing so hard they had to sit down holding their sides.

Chuckling to himself, Ron put down his coffee, opened his laptop, and began the arduous task of looking for a job, figuring he would start with the government's job bank.

Finding the official website, he scrolled down the job openings, many of which were not what he was looking for. Construction worker, farmer, dental assistant, chaplain—Ron smiled at the last result, as Dad could probably be qualified for that job.

When he typed in "business" to narrow down the search, the results began to match Ron's criteria better. He saw several postings for business managers and business analysts.

As he read through the requirements of some of the positions, it became apparent that a lack of experience was going to drastically limit his chances of getting a high-end professional job—at least until he got more working experience.

Scanning through the results, he noticed a listing for a manager of a utility company in Burnaby called BC Electric. They even had a corny slogan: "Let's em-power you." Chuckling at the use of the pun, he figured the company at least had a sense of humour.

Saving the page, Ron continued browsing the endless list

of opportunities, but he felt confident the ad for BC Electric was the best opportunity to apply for.

When he looked at his watch, he saw it was nearly time to go to badminton practice for the Canada team. After packing his gym clothes and grabbing his rackets and bag, he waved goodbye to his parents and headed off for the Richmond Dome.

As he drove past the Oak Street Bridge, traffic slowed to a crawl and the heat of the midday sun was scorching hot. All around him, people were not in the best of attitudes, and there was a constant sound of drivers blaring their horns in frustration.

Turning on his air conditioning, he felt the cold, refreshing breeze cool his burning face. Meanwhile, the sun blared intense heat onto his skin, and his farmer's tan was evident as he rested his arm in the open window.

Pulling into the makeshift badminton facility, Ron shouldered his bag. He was five minutes early—giving him enough time to change to his nonmarking court shoes.

"Here comes all-rounder Ron!" said Steve as he noticed Ron entering the gym. It was their nickname for him, as he was a fairly skilled player in all the techniques of badminton.

Returning the greeting, Ron hid his dislike of pet names and played along. "Hey, Smashing Steve!" he called out. Ironically, Steve wasn't good at smashing, but that was one of the only techniques that started with an *s*.

"Is Coach not here yet?" Ron asked.

Lucy shook her head as she answered Ron. "Nah, he's over there helping Xu with his serve. Come on, let's rally."

Pang pang! The sound of the shuttle being viciously attacked by the rackets echoed across the walls of the gym. Feinting a clear, missing the birdie at head height, then bringing the racket like an undercut, Ron put the birdie across the net in a perfect drop shot.

"No trick shots, Ron!" Coach shook his head disapprovingly. "If I see you trying a stunt like that in a real game, I'll pull your sorry behind to the bench."

Ron apologized with a slight nod and continued rallying the shuttle across the net. Apart from Lucy and himself, who were playing singles, everyone else had a partner to play with. He had tried doubles, but the process of relying on someone always tangled up his thoughts, forcing him to be unable to focus on the game. But in singles, he didn't need to rely on a partner, making it only his fault if he lost—but also his credit if he won.

Pang Ssnnnaappp!

Ron held his racket sheepishly, showing the broken string near the top of the racket.

"I told you twenty-five pounds of tension was too much. You should listen to me next time," Steve said as he took out his scissors and helped cut the rest of the strings to relieve the tension. With the strings relaxed, the frame of the racket reformed back into the shape of a round oval.

"Well, Xu uses thirty," Ron said. "Why is it only my strings that break?" Putting the broken racket back, he took out a new one—one of three that he usually carried to practice and games.

"It's because you're picking up the birdies with your racket. When you scoop them up, the strings on the sides get worn out quickly," the coach explained.

"Thanks, Coach, I'll try and pick them up by hand."

Chuckling to himself, the veteran badminton player warned Ron about being overly sure of himself. "Old habits die hard. Remember that, bud."

As if on cue, Ron started to pick up a shuttle with his racket, but at the last second held back and bent down to pick it up. Indeed, his coach was right. He thought that perhaps the thirty-dollar repair bill would motivate him to change that. Breaking a racket every two weeks was expensive in an already expensive year, and he had only a small amount of savings left after grad school tuition.

Dictating the rally, Ron had a knack for finding the right opportunity to attack while at the same time having a strong defence to wait for that perfect chance. By the end of the rally, Lucy was gulping for air, bent over double and holding her hand out to signal she needed to rest a bit. Ron, on the other hand, was calm and composed even though his body was screaming that it was tired. He pushed on, ignoring the pain.

In the change room, everyone put back on their casual attire, and it was evident that some of the team liked flashy, bright-coloured clothing. Ron donned a white hoodie and khaki shorts, while Xu wore the ugliest Hawaiian shirt that seemed to commit every fashion sin there was.

Trying desperately not to laugh at the shirt, Ron said goodbye to the team and headed out, eager to make the afternoon dim sum cut-off time at his favourite restaurant.

"*Sui mie, hah gow, yiew chee gow.*" The waitress called out the popular Cantonese Chinese dishes as she pushed a food cart around a small dining room.

Soon enough, Ron was enjoying the delicious food in a variety of dishes, much of which his dad couldn't eat—hence he opted to eat alone and not make Dad uncomfortable.

Seeing his favourite dessert come by, he flagged down the waiter. "I'll take one plate of *dan tat mm gwoi*," he said. The waiter winced at his half English and half butchered Chinese, but smiling, he gave Ron a plate of three egg tarts and stamped the bill. Devouring his dessert, Ron saved the other two for his parents, knowing his dad also enjoyed them. Dad liked the Portuguese-style versions, while Mom savoured the flaky-crusted normal ones.

Driving along Marine Drive, Ron enjoyed the scenes of

the river, as tugboats and cargo ships sailed to and fro. Taking a left turn, he opted for Highway 1 and the Port Mann Bridge rather than the old and poorly maintained Pattullo Bridge.

Passing under the ginormous cables holding up the Port Mann, Ron remembered the winter several years earlier when ice bombarded cars on the bridge, causing mayhem. Indeed, his mom's car was hit by a smaller piece, but fortunately no damage was done.

Arriving home, he saw a familiar car in the driveway—a yellow sedan with a Texas license plate. There was a dent on the rear-left passenger door and a baby seat in the back seat.

Walking in the door, Ron saw someone he hadn't wanted to ever see again: his sister.

CHAPTER 10

REUNION

"Say Ma Ma, Ma Ma. Good girl." Ron's sister, Euodia, was coaxing her daughter to greet her grandma.

Hearing the front door shut, she caught sight of Ron heading up the stairs, trying to remain unnoticed.

"Aaron. Ron, please—"

Bang!

Ron's door closed with a familiar crash, as it had done hundreds of times while the siblings were growing up. Six years apart had made little difference in how Ron felt about his older sister. Indeed, she had changed much, and she had led Dad to become religious. And Ron figured she was now trying to make him believe as well. All he knew was that from a young age, she had mocked, hit, and ridiculed him throughout his childhood, and he had no intention of letting it go, no matter how much she had changed.

Knock knock.

"Aaron? Aaron, it's me, Euodia. Look, can we talk please?"

Dad pleaded to Ron on behalf of Euodia. "Honey, she's your sister. Please, just—"

"Go away! I don't want to talk to her."

"I got a gift for you, Aaron. I know you don't want to talk to me, and I don't blame you, considering all the wrongs I've done to you. You can hate me all you want, but please, if you give me a chance, I'd like to apologize for my actions—"

Thump!

The sound of something heavy thrown at the door signalled that Ron was going to stop listening.

As he lay on his bed, he wished his sister would just leave him alone. *Euodia*. That name was enough to make his blood boil. It didn't matter that she'd changed. He admitted she was different—more caring, less abusive, and less manipulative before moving to Texas six years earlier. But it would be unfair to forget all her faults just because she'd developed a conscience. How could he simply let slide every abuse she'd ever inflicted on him?

To him, his sister was a perpetual enemy, the clearest example of how the people who are closest to you are the ones who hurt you the most. He and Euodia had fought most of their lives over leftovers, Halloween candy, and even video games. Like oil and water, they just couldn't get along; Ron even wondered how they could even be related. Having her hundreds of kilometres away in Texas had given him much-needed breathing room. But his peaceful existence now lay broken, thanks to the timely intrusion of his sister.

Walking back into the kitchen and leaving Ron alone, the family discussed Ron's condition. "He's been doing alright," Dad explained. "He was devastated when his girlfriend passed away. But for the most part, he's been able to move on."

"That's good to hear. I regret being so harsh with him when we were younger. I doubt he'll ever forgive me. I just wish I'd been kinder to him."

As Euodia held Dad's hands, they both prayed silently for Ron and his well-being. Though they knew restoring a relationship was a long shot, they also knew anything was possible.

After everyone was asleep, Ron quietly slipped out and into his car. His anger and stress had built up throughout that day thanks to his sister, so he'd decided to train at the gym to let out some steam.

Driving past a police car, he noticed a large van was stopped and the officer was writing a ticket for the driver. The motto on the van was "Rent a Van-couver." Ron laughed as he shook his head, thinking it was one of the worst mottos he'd ever seen.

Pulling up at the gym, he was relieved there appeared to be no one inside, allowing him to work in silence. Also, given it was ten at night, Ron felt more comfortable exercising alone without someone creepy watching him.

Pummeling the punching bag, he vented all his frustration in a barrage of fists. Resting for a moment, he noticed his knuckles were sore from the jabs, but he forgot the pain in his rage. Moving on to the foot press, he lifted nearly two hundred pounds with his legs, keeping his mind on training, instead of remembering Euodia. He got angrier every time he thought of her.

Breathing heavily, Ron rested, wiping down the equipment. Beads of sweat dripped onto the floor, like the many tears he'd shed after being bullied by Euodia. By the time he finished his workout, it was raining outside, coating the streets with a thin layer of water that glimmered and shone from the reflections of the streetlamps. The eerie silence of downtown Cloverdale in the downpour was both peaceful and dangerous, calming yet unrelenting.

Letting the rain cool him down, he stood for a minute before getting into his car. Once he got in, he turned on the radio to the classical music channel and drove off into the downpour, listening to some baroque music.

As he parked the car, the sun was just starting to peek over the horizon, casting an orangey-golden sky over the land, with one or two lazy rainclouds still floating around. Absorbing the first rays of sunshine, Ron sat there for a moment as the birds started their morning songs. Thinking it was about time to face the fireworks, he walked up to the house and was about to open the door when someone opened it from the inside.

Seeing Euodia, he solemnly walked slowly past, not thanking her or greeting her. He just walked in dead silence.

"Aaron, Mom made breakfast if you want some. There's scrambled eggs, waffles, and sausage. This is Bill, my husband, and this little girl here is my daughter, Chloe."

Ron looked at the toddler without any expression, grabbed a plate with breakfast, and walked up the stairs after a nod of thanks to Mom.

The tension in the room was suffocating, and the awkwardness of the silence made everyone uncomfortable. Even baby Chloe started whimpering shortly after seeing Ron.

"There, there. Aw, that's okay, don't cry." Euodia cradled her daughter and comforted her.

Ron went into his room and, after shutting the door, noticed a package on his desk. Putting down the breakfast, he took the package and read a note attached to it:

> To my dear brother Aaron,
>
> Words can't express how sorry I am for treating you as I did in our childhood. You don't have to forgive me, but I hope this gift will help you heal, just as it helped me heal from my past as well.
>
> Yours, Euodia

Ron put down the note and carefully unwrapped the

package. Inside was a leather book with golden edges on the pages and a golden bookmark. It wasn't hard to guess what book it was, knowing his sister and her new beliefs she had accepted nearly seven years before. Putting the gift down, he looked at the one picture in his room that had his sister in it. It was a family portrait done when he was four. Mother sat in the chair, while he and his sister were on either side of her. Dad looked on from the back, leaning on the chair. Ron remembered that when that photo was taken, he and his sister were arguing about who should be on Mom's right-hand side.

Trying to quell his curiosity about his new book, Ron put it in the darkness of a drawer in his desk, shutting it angrily. *Good riddance,* he thought.

Listening intently, he could hear the muffled discussions of his family—his father's monotonous, caring voice, along with a worried tone from his sister.

He watched as a ladybug tried to crawl outside, trapped by the window. Its frantic scurrying back and forth proved fruitless as it became more desperate. Knowing the insect would die if it could not escape, Ron opened the window and let the ladybug out—setting the poor insect free.

Meanwhile, at the kitchen table, a family meeting was being held. Euodia and her husband, Bill, were contemplating how long they should stay and whether they should stay at a hotel to keep tensions low with Ron.

"Mom, we don't mind living in a hotel, if it's for the best. We don't want to cause trouble for Ron."

"Euodia, a hotel is expensive!" Mom said. "Plus, it's a hassle to take care of a baby at a hotel. Here we can help you look after Chloe. Ron will come around. He's changed much if you give him enough time to prove it."

"Your mom's right. If you're at a hotel, you'll miss the opportunity to make up with Ron," Dad added. "Avoiding the problem won't fix it. We have to fix our attention on our goals and not compromise or settle for anything less. Not to mention, you haven't tried my famous hazelnut banana bread. It's definitely worth staying for."

"That's about the only thing you can bake that's good, dear." Mom patted Dad's back pretending to pity him.

Dad laughed. "Your mother knows I'm a good cook. She just won't admit it. Yowch!" Mother had taken hold of Dad's ear and was gently yanking it like she was warning a pet dog.

"Dad, you just always know what to say to embarrass Mom, don't you?" The familiar voice caused everyone to turn around in surprise as Ron walked into the meeting. Euodia offered a hug to him. He resisted at first but then hesitantly hugged her back.

"I can't forget everything you did against me, but for the sake of Mom and Dad, I'm open to making amends," he said.

Dad grinned at the change in his son's attitude, and indeed it was infectious, as soon the entire family was grinning, smiling, and laughing at the deescalated tension.

In fact, everyone was so happy with the rekindled relationship spark within the family that Mom ordered pizza once again—but this time four large pizzas instead of three, to accommodate the new mouths to feed. There was a Hawaiian pizza for Mom, two vegetarians for both Ron and Euodia's family, and one deep-dish cheese pizza for Dad, with cheesy crusts.

Ron watched as Chloe gobbled down a portion of pizza—a silly grin betraying just how much the toddler was enjoying the food. Bill wiped a piece of tomato sauce from his daughter's cheek, and Ron grinned at the little girl's behaviour.

"Here, Chloe, have some pepper—" Bill started to say.

"Bill, wait! That's jalapeño!" Euodia pulled Chloe away from the pepper just in the nick of time. "Careful, it's too spicy for her, dear."

Ron promptly ate the pepper previously destined for Chloe. "It's not spicy at all! See?" He opened his mouth, showing he'd eaten it all. "Perfectly fine for me."

"Just like your mother," Dad said. "You burned all your tastebuds in your youth—now you can't taste any heat. It's called desensitization, Son."

"Well, at least we're courageous enough to try spicy food, unlike someone we know." Mom winked at Ron, darting her eyes towards Dad.

"I don't miss a thing—the only spice I need is you, dear," Dad said as he planted a wet kiss on her cheek.

Mom wiped it off, blushing. "Away from me, you salty sea dog. Your whiskers prick! Why don't you shave anymore?"

"Doesn't it make me more handsome? Euodia, what do you think about your papa's facial hair?"

"I agree with Mom. Clean-shaven is better, Pops."

Crestfallen, Dad shook his head. "Women have no appreciation for rustic character nowadays."

Chuckling to himself, Ron patted Dad on the back. "It's okay, Dad, don't worry. Mom's hiding what she wants. I'll bet she likes your beard."

"You think so? I've worked quite hard to grow this stubble—not to mention maintaining it and grooming it as well."

Hiding a nostalgic look on his face, Ron recalled a memory. "Penny once told me she liked your beard. That's how I know."

His dad placed a caring hand on his son's shoulders, as if helping carry the heavy burden of loss his son had to endure. In his heart, Dad was happy with how his son was dealing with everything—how he was moving on after losing Penny, making amends with his sister, and even playing sports.

"I'm really glad we had you as a son," Dad said. "And your sister as well. It wasn't always easy with you two, but we're happy how you two have turned out. Not raw, not overcooked, but a perfect medium rare."

"Should we be happy that you're relating us to steaks?" Euodia asked.

"Sis, of course it makes sense. We're beefy, juicy, and well-seasoned—just like a steak!" Ron replied.

"You two are out of your minds. Mom, don't you agree?" Euodia said.

"Hmm, what's that dear?" Mom pretended not to hear, to avoid getting involved in the increasingly embarrassing situation.

Euodia rolled her eyes and lamented, "It seems I'm the only normal person in this family. Alright, where do you want these extra slices, Mom?" Mom pointed at the fridge, and Euodia stacked the pieces of pizza together and put them in the fridge, away from Chloe, who was starting to nod off into slumber.

Picking up their sleeping daughter, Euodia and Bill retreated to the guest room to prepare for the night and tuck her into bed.

Ron spent a few minutes looking at the aquarium, trying to find the third ghost shrimp that should have been in the tank. Either it had been eaten or somehow escaped the tank. Dropping in a little bit of flake fish food, he watched the fish gobble it all down as if there had been a famine in the tank. Giving up hope trying to find the third shrimp, Ron also retired, getting ready for bed.

Dad helped Mom finish the dishes and wiped the table down until it was spic-and-span.

"Thanks for the help, hon, I'll finish up here," Mom finally said.

Dad nodded, gave her a kiss goodnight, and headed upstairs like his son and daughter.

Mom finished drying the dishes, then washed the hand

towels and hung them out to dry. Taking out some frozen chicken, she put it in the fridge to defrost overnight. Lastly, she took Ron's shorts that had a button loose and sewed it back tight with a needle and thread, showing the prowess of a master seamstress. After brushing up, she carefully crawled into bed, so as not to wake her husband, and turned off her light, finishing yet another day—ready for the next one to come.

Indeed, Mom was eagerly ready for the next day, being the first to wake up. She started making breakfast as the rest of the family stumbled into the kitchen—attracted by the delicious aroma of food being cooked and coffee being brewed.

Euodia started helping Mom, setting the plates and cutlery on the table, while baby Chloe watched hungrily.

Starting with Dad's portion so that there wouldn't be any cross-contamination with pork, Mom made an omelet with sautéed onions and chicken.

Euodia was in charge of the toast, spreading it thick with peanut butter and strawberry jam.

While daughter and mother worked, the men kept busy talking about the news, praising their women in their thoughts for their hard work.

Served pancakes with sausage and bacon, Ron drowned his with syrup until his plate resembled a pool of sweet molasses. Baby Chloe, seeing her uncle, reached for the syrup as well, attempting to do the same to her pancakes. But Euodia put the syrup out of hands' reach for Chloe and enticed her daughter with a piece of bacon to make her forget the syrup. Soon, Chloe was completely preoccupied with the bacon and forgot all about the syrup, chowing down on the deliciously crunchy strips of meat.

Dad, on the other hand, poured ketchup onto his omelet, drowning it just as Ron did with his syrup. Mom looked at

Ron's sea of syrup and Dad's pool of ketchup. Speechless, she shook her head in disbelief. "Like father, like son," she said. She didn't even bother chiding her son and husband anymore.

Both Ron and Dad smiled sheepishly and looked guiltily at Mom, like children caught red-handed.

After breakfast, Euodia and Bill decided to take Chloe to the aquarium with Dad, while Ron decided to look at some old picture albums in the office, hoping to find some embarrassing pictures of Euodia. Gazing at an old picture of Mom at the hospital with her baby bump, he smiled; Mom and Dad looked so happy. As he was turning the page, he noticed a small photo in between the photos on either side. Carefully sliding it out, he found a small photo of a baby. Thinking it was either him or Euodia, he looked at the back and noticed the baby's name was Daniel and that he was born on November 22, 1990, earlier than his sister by four years. Sliding the fragile photo back between the joyous photos of Mom and Dad, Ron now understood why there was another baby photo. Mom had lost a baby before he and Euodia were born.

Walking downstairs to Mom, he found her busily washing the dishes left over from breakfast. Giving her a big hug, he wondered how she could have hidden such grief from him and his sister.

Holding on to Mom's hand, Ron struggled to figure out how best to tell her that he knew. "Mom, uh, I found out about Daniel." He looked down at his feet, feeling embarrassed at exposing Mom and Dad's secret.

Mom froze, not moving at all for a second, before turning around and giving Ron a soapy hug, tears threatening to roll down her face.

"I'm here, Mom. Don't worry, I'm here." Patting her back, Ron held his mother in his arms, astonished as years of grief held back in her heart came gushing out in torrents.

A few hours later, Dad and the rest of the family bumbled back, laughing and reminding each other of the wonders of the aquatic life at the aquarium.

Dad, seeing Mom's tearstained face, stopped laughing immediately and asked her what was wrong, giving her a tender hug.

"Dad, I found out about Daniel," Ron said.

All the laughter and joy of just seconds before vanished into thin air as Dad held on to Mom, who was continuously sobbing.

"Who's Daniel?" Euodia was confused as to what this was about.

"Daniel was our older brother, Euodia. But Mom and Dad lost him when he was a baby."

"Oh, Mom ..." Euodia also went over to comfort Mom, hugging her closely.

Baby Chloe walked over to Mom and held her hand, wondering why her grandmother was crying. "Mah mah?" she said.

Mom looked at Chloe through the tears and half smiled, picking her up and gently brushing her hair.

Feeling guilty that he had reminded his parents of this tragedy, Ron decided that at least he and Euodia would be able to comfort them in their sorrow, which was no longer a secret. Thinking back to the pictures of Mom and Dad happily bringing two more babies into the world, he wondered how worried they might have been, having experienced such loss in the past. Their hidden anxiety and grief were overshadowed by their joy and excitement, their sadness concealed by smiling, beaming faces.

"So, what did you see at the aquarium today, Chloe?" Mom's voice trembled as she held back her emotions.

"Big fish!" Little Chloe spread out her hands as far as she could, indicating how big the fish was. "Berry big fish!"

"A berry big fish, eh?" Ron couldn't help but smile. "Did the berry big fish try to eat you?"

A face of mock horror formed on Chloe's face as she imagined being eaten by the fish. "Mommy! Chloe don't want to be eated!"

"Don't listen to Uncle Ron. Big fishes only eat little children who misbehave."

"Chloe be good, Chloe be good, no eated by fish," the little girl said solemnly.

"I've heard that good children go to bed early, without having their parents tell them to—"

Before Ron could finish, Chloe pretended to fall asleep, making small snoring noises.

The whole family laughed at the little child's clever antics and temporarily forgot the sadness brought about by a long-lost memory.

Having tucked Chloe into bed, Mom took out a box and put it on the table. She gently pulled out a blue toque so small it fit into her palm. Next came a pair of light-blue socks, petite enough to have been for some small animal or dog. The family then looked at several pocket photos of Mom affectionately holding Daniel. He was so tiny, and Mom had a maternally proud grin on her face. Another photo showed Dad with his wife and son, but his slightly worried expression couldn't be unnoticed.

"So where was ... Where was Daniel laid to rest?" Ron asked, though the question seemed awkward and untimely, and the silent pause made everyone uncomfortable.

"His memorial plaque is in a cemetery park in Vancouver. In between two giant spruce trees. We could plan a visit, if that's okay with Mom," Dad said, looking with concern at Mom.

"We can go. We haven't been in a while," she said.

Euodia put a hand on Mom's shoulder, reassuring her they didn't have to if she didn't feel up to it. "We don't have to if you don't want to, Mom. Are you sure?"

"Yes, yes. We should go."

Dad wrapped his arm around her, kissing her cheek affectionately.

The next morning, they started the road trip, and the drive to Vancouver was solemn. Little was heard and even less was said, as everyone knew laughter and happiness were, for the time being, grossly out of place. Even little Chloe opted not to giggle or play, sensing the seriousness of the situation.

Arriving at the cemetery, they silently walked towards a grove of trees that broke the horizon of a well-cared-for lawn.

Ron looked at the variety of tombstones—some large, some small—wondering what kind of memorial had been given to baby Daniel. And upon arriving at the site, he and his sister finally met the burial place of their older brother.

A small plaque made of bronze, which had turned slightly green, marked the spot, with orange and brown pine needles lying around the plaque. Little Chloe put a small rose near the memorial, as instructed by her mom, and after a still and awkward silence, they began to walk away.

Ron thought about what having an older brother would have been like, and he wasn't sure if he would have liked having another elder sibling. Nonetheless, he felt sorry for his parents, and he recognized their courage to keep trying, ultimately succeeding in bringing two more children into the world.

Back at home, the bustle of daily life continued, as Ron followed through with a job listing at the local utility company. The company offered benefits, including medical and dental, and a jaw-dropping wage of twenty-eight dollars an hour.

He applied for the position and hoped to get an interview with the prestigious company.

Euodia and Bill planned to stay for one more week before heading back to Texas, where Chloe was to start preschool after the summer break.

One night, the entire family was playing a board game, where players build hotels and charge each other rent. To the family's surprise, Mom earned the most in revenue and ultimately bankrupted everyone else, winning the game.

"This game is so unfair!" Ron exclaimed. "I bet the dice are loaded. I'm serious! Mom rolled twelve nearly ten times!"

"It's all in the wrist, Ron," Mom insisted. "If you roll properly, you'll get a higher chance of getting the number you want. See, watch." Mom promptly rolled yet another pair of sixes as proof that she wasn't lying.

Ron rolled his eyes. "Our mother's the master of games of chance. Remind me not to play another board game with her."

"You know, your mother is also a pro at billiards, Ping-Pong, cards, and marbles. It was her skill at billiards that sparked our relationship, you know," Dad said.

Mom laughed. "I remember, you challenged me to a game of billiards. I said that if you won, I'd go on a coffee date with you."

Embarrassed, Dad hid his face behind the newspaper.

Ron chuckled. "Who won, then?"

"I outplayed him and he lost terribly," Mom said, laughing. "But I still went on that date with him."

"How did you know I didn't let you win, my dear?" Dad plastered a grin on his face, looking at Mother mischievously.

"If I recall, when you lost you said, 'Let's make it the best out of three.'"

Dad hid his face even further.

"And I promptly beat him again, winning two out of three."

Dad's injured pride was so comical that everyone burst out laughing, and Dad's ears turned bright red in embarrassment.

Back upstairs in his room, Ron checked his email and read a reply from the utility company:

> Dear Mr. Lee
>
> We have received your application and would like to move forward with an interview sometime this week. Please let us know what time you'd be available to come in for an interview.
>
> BC Electric Human Resources
>
> J. Horg

The next day, Dad wondered why Ron rushed out so fast after wolfing down his breakfast.

"He got an interview?" he said in response to Mom's answer. "I thought he just applied yesterday." Dad was surprised at the prompt reply from the company.

"That's what he said," Mom insisted. "The interview's going to be this afternoon. He ran off before telling me more. I just hope he's not late or anything."

"It's great to see him so excited again. Getting a job would help his self-esteem. What doesn't kill you only makes you stronger. But honestly, there were times I thought he was going to … Going to … You know. Give up."

Mom nodded in agreement, then busied herself preparing for lunch.

Meanwhile, Ron was racing to be on time for his interview at BC Electric. Flying down 64th Avenue at the maximum speed limit, he was brimming with adrenaline, eager to get his first job interview. Parking the car, he took a mint for his breath and took a second to compose himself before heading towards the main building and office.

Entering the air-conditioned building, Ron walked up to the reception desk and checked in. "I'm here to see Mr. Horg for an interview?"

"What's your name and what time is your appointment?" asked the receptionist.

"Ron Lee. I'm here for a twelve-thirty appointment."

"Alright, please have a seat. I'll let Mr. Horg know you're waiting."

Several minutes later, Mr. Horg came out and asked Ron to come in. Walking through a hallway full of acrylic paintings, they entered a small office with a breathtaking view of Burnaby. "Take a seat Ron. Thank you for coming for the interview. If you can give me a second, I'll pull out your resume." Mr. Horg went through some papers on his desk. "So, I see you graduated from Stikine University with a master's in business. When did you graduate?"

"I got my degree this year, actually, after the spring semester."

"I see. Unfortunately, that means you're quite new and don't have much work experience in this field, I take it?"

"Yes, you're right. But I did graduate with honours, with a GPA of 4.0."

"Do you have any requirements that you wish to make known before we consider your application formally?"

"I was briefed with the description of the job, so I'm fine with what the job entails as well as its compensation and benefits."

"Good, good. Now usually we screen for candidates one or two years in advance, but this position currently is in dire need of a suitable candidate, hence the urgency of our hiring process. Lastly, just as a final question, are you a team player? Because everyone here must work together as a team, relying on one another. Are you fine with that?"

"Yes, I do consider myself a team player, very much so."

"That's excellent. Well, we'll consider your application with the others. If anything comes up, we'll let you know. It was nice to meet you, Ron."

"Thank you, Mr. Horg, I look forward to seeing you again. Bye."

Leaving the office, Ron had a spring in his step and held his head high. He was brimming with confidence as he wondered what life would be like working for such a big, well-regarded, and prestigious company.

When he arrived back home, Mom and Dad saw him beaming, with a smile so large it would have rivalled a crocodile's grin.

"How did the interview go? Well, I hope?" Dad raised an eyebrow—probing his son.

"I think I did okay, the only problem was I didn't have as much experience as they would have wanted," Ron told him. "I just hope my education can compensate for the lack of experience."

"Which position did you apply for, Ron? Don't worry about taking a lower position. Getting a foot in the door is all you need. You can always move up over time," advised Mom.

Shaking his head, Dad refuted Mom's expectations of moving up, reassuring Ron that any job position is a good one. "What's wrong with a lower position permanently? As long as you work hard and do your best, that's what counts, my son. Higher positions are nice but don't necessarily equate to contentment."

Mom pouted as her advice was brushed aside, so she

busied herself with preparing lunch, mumbling something about husbands being too easygoing.

"Where's Euodia and Bill? Did they go sightseeing with Chloe?" Ron asked, looking around and noticing the lack of commotion and noise.

"We suggested they go to the suspension bridge in North Vancouver, so they'll likely be gone for a few more hours," Mom said. "Do you want some coffee?"

Imitating a British accent, Ron said, "Please, ma'am, I want some more."

"Aw, my poor little orphan boy. Here you go." Mom poured the aromatic coffee for Ron and watched in horror as her son put in four tablespoons of sugar. "Ron! That's way too much sugar! You'll get diabetes!"

"Don't worry, Mom, it's just the way I like it," Ron said, laughing.

Dad put on a face of innocence. "He didn't get that from my side of the family."

"Oh? And pray, who was using a whole bottle of ketchup for a single omelet?" Mom had the smuggest smirk as she tsked her husband and son. "It couldn't have been my dear, innocent husband. Perhaps it was a kitchen bandit?"

"Hmph." Dad went back into his paper, muttering something about wives and smart alecks.

Trying desperately not to pick a side, Ron took his coffee and headed upstairs, holding the coffee in perfect balance, with not a single drop spilt. Taking a sip, he opened his laptop and started sifting through his emails.

Then a single email caught his eye. It was sent by Penny.

His hand shaking, he clicked open the email and noticed a brief intro had been inserted by Penny's parents:

This email was meant to be sent to you by Penny, but she never had the chance to send it. We hope you will understand she cared a lot for you.

Sorry for taking so long to send it to you.

Ron took a breath before reading the rest of the letter:

My dearest Ron,

I know you are devastated about not making grad school, that your health is not its best, and that you're stuck in a hospital. But I'm here for you, as are your parents, so don't feel you are all alone. Remember what I said about being content rather than resenting what you have in life. I know I sound like a broken record playing the same thing over and over. But it is true. I look forward to playing mixed doubles badminton with you again in the near future.

Keep your head up, my boy.

Yours truly,

Penny

A single tear welled up in Ron's eye as every emotional scar and wound ripped right open. It hurt, but once again it was starting to heal, but way deeper than before. Hearing the hustle downstairs, he knew his sister and her family had returned. So, wiping his tears away, he walked downstairs with a façade-like smile, making sure not to reveal his inner turmoil.

"The bridge was so wobbly. It was a good thing Chloe was strapped to your back, Bill. Otherwise, she might have fallen off!" Euodia was saying as Ron approached the room.

"Chloe, what do you think? Did you like the big bridge?" Mom tickled the little girl's chin.

Chloe giggled in response.

"She enjoyed it for sure," Bill said. "She probably had the best view, too, on my poor back."

"I guess we don't need pack mules," Euodia said. "A husband can carry everything! Although a mule only needs to eat grass. What do you say, Chloe? Should we trade Daddy for a donkey?"

Chloe was confused by the question, not quite understanding it, and Bill looked annoyed at his wife's sarcasm.

"Ron!" Euodia said when he walked into the room. "Mom and Dad said you just went for an interview with BC Electric? Congratulations, Brother! We're so happy for you."

Ron hugged his sister, glad to get his mind off the email Penny had written. "Good things come to those who wait, I guess ..." he said, his voice trailing off to nothing.

"If you get the job, Ron, we'll order pizza!" Mom said.

Dad made a face of sheer surprise. "My, my, is this my wife talking? Pizza twice in less than a month? Alright, where did my health-fanatic wife go? Who are you, stranger?"

Mom made a smug smile to rebuke her husband's silliness. "One more word out of you, dear, and there'll be no pizza for you."

Dad's sarcasm turned into mock horror and repentance. "Oh, wonderful wife," he said, "I shall close my mouth and not speak another word to your displeasure, Your Highness."

"Good, at least we'll have some peace and quiet now. What on earth—" Mom exclaimed as Dad grabbed her hand and kept kissing it.

Looking away in embarrassment, Euodia sighed, shaking her head. Meanwhile, Ron tried his best not to burst out laughing at his parents' theatrics.

"I'm so glad you and I are much more well-behaved, don't you think—" Euodia barely finished her thought before Bill started kissing her hand too. "Oh no! Not you too, Bill!"

That was too much for Ron. He burst out laughing at both his dad and brother-in-law, not stopping until his sides ached.

"You guys are like lovesick puppies," Ron said while laughing. In fact, he laughed so hard he started crying, but they were tears of joy in contrast to the tears of sadness he'd wept just moments before.

CHAPTER 11

CHAMPION

"Keep clearing, Ron!" Coach Lucas kept feeding shots for Ron to clear, alternating between a forehand and backhand clear. "Back, all the way back. Make sure it reaches the backline."

Ron's arm was getting sore, but he pushed on, knowing that practice was needed if he was to compete successfully on the national team.

The Richmond Dome built for the 2010 Sports Competition was a beautiful structure, with sunlight filtering through the windows into the gym and casting rays of light, which revealed the dust motes floating around.

"Make sure you're using that wrist, Ron, and hit the shuttle at the highest point you can to make it go as far as possible," the coach said.

After each clear, Ron positioned his racket behind his back, and as he rotated his body, he stretched his arm as well, pronating his wrist to hit the birdie with as much force as he could. He watched as the birdie flew sky-high, then like a missile, fell and landed about a foot from the end line.

"Not bad, keep it up." With the coach's encouragement,

Ron kept trying his best to successfully perform a perfect clear, but it appeared that much practice would be needed to accomplish that feat.

"Alright, have a rest, Ron. Lucy, you're up!"

Ron sat down, exhausted, on the bleachers. Then he, along with Xu and Steve, watched the rest of the team practicing. "How do you think we'll do at the Sports Competition?" Ron asked while still mildly gasping for air.

"I'd say we have a fair chance of reaching the round of thirty-two. It depends on our matchups, you know," said Xu as he spun his racket in his hand.

STEVE, however, was confident in their team, giving his prediction as a matter of fact. "The Sports Competition is still six months away; we'll have to train super hard if we want to get past the second round. Honestly, I think our best chances are with you and our women's doubles."

Ron looked over at the women's doubles team training as a pair and said, "You guys really think me, Michelle and Rachel have a chance? I'd be happy just by winning our first match and not striking out on the first day."

The three of them didn't notice the coach walking up beside them, hearing their conversation.

"The best attitude to have is to play for fun, no matter if you win or lose. Expectations can be devastating; the secret is to enjoy your games," the coach said. "Focus on releasing yourselves from those restrictive expectations, then you'll be able to play your best game, and that's what counts."

A bit startled at having their coach sneak up on them, the trio bobbed their heads in agreement, slightly embarrassed.

"Alright, back to work boys, enough resting." He signalled them to take the far court, and they started rallying back and forth.

"Let's work on our net shots. That alright, Ron?" said Steve.

Ron gave a thumbs-up, walked towards the net, and told Steve to start. "Sounds good, let's do it."

With both sides standing at the net, they began dropping the birdie just over the net while trying to put a spin on it to make it harder for the opponent to return. Pretty soon, the entire team was exhausted from the workout, and Coach Lucas gathered everyone together to make an announcement.

"Okay, gang. Good work training, everyone. I just wanted to announce that we've qualified to enter every badminton discipline at the Tokyo Sports Competition in July! Congratulations, team! Give yourselves a pat on the back."

Everyone hooted and shouted out in surprise at the good news.

"Please check your schedules and make sure you can allocate enough time to participate in the games in mid-July. Well done, everyone. That's all. Dismissed."

In the change room, the Sports Competition was all everyone talked about. Surprise, excitement, and pride were mixed with relief and satisfaction with the amount of hard work that the whole team had put in.

"Imagine, guys, playing in front of hundreds of people. Just thinking about it makes me nervous," Ron said.

"Ron, don't forget what the coach said. Don't pen yourself into expectations. Rather, release your restrictions," Steve said.

"It's kind of hard not to feel the pressure to do well," Ron replied. "I mean, our country is depending on us, watching us represent them. How can we ignore the expectations the country puts on us?"

Steve took a minute, contemplating an answer, but couldn't think of a response.

"Perhaps by understanding that your country just wants you to do your best to represent them instead of thinking they want more medals," Xu said.

"Xu's right," Steve replied. "Medals are important, but the effort is what counts. Just try your best and leave the rest to luck."

Ron shook his head. "There's no such thing as luck. Something I learned a long time ago. You can have all the luck in the world, but you won't be successful if you don't train and work hard. Sheer determination and ambition outweigh any luck there may be."

"That's where you're wrong, Ron. What about net cords, frame hits, or between-the-leg shots? You can't practice those, yet they happen and can change the course of a game." It almost seemed like Xu was lecturing Ron in a motivational speech.

Ron pondered for a moment, then shrugged. "My sister and her family are leaving today, so I gotta get a farewell gift for them. Gotta go. See you guys tomorrow!"

Browsing the gift shop, he wanted to give Euodia something she would remember him by. He couldn't believe that in three short weeks, his relationship with his sister had improved so much. Picking up a snow globe, he reasoned the snow in it would help Euodia remember Vancouver and Canada when they went back to sunny Texas. Inside the globe was a snow goose with her gosling, seemingly oblivious to the artificial snow falling all around them.

Back at home, Euodia and her family were preparing to leave, and Ron just had enough time to give his farewell gift.

"Ron, I really hope you get the job at BC Electric, and when you do, give us a call, eh? Bill and I would be extremely proud and happy for you," Euodia said. "Also, thanks so much for the snow globe, we've got a perfect place for it on the mantle."

"Goodbye, Chloe, your Uncle Ron will come visit you guys soon, okay?" Ron said.

All buckled up in the car seat, Chloe waved politely at him before looking back to the tablet that she had been playing with

Euodia and Bill waved goodbye as well as they entered their car and drove away, their Texas license plate slightly slanted to the left.

Ron waved back, and by chance, caught sight of a new apple growing from the tree in the front yard. The late spring bloom of flowers had begun to bear fruit, and just as Ron and Euodia had healed their relationship, they would soon harvest a bumper crop of memories they had made during the brief summer together.

Having said goodbye, Ron then told his parents the good news that his team qualified for the Sports Competition.

"We're so happy for you, Ron! Will you be on live TV? You're going to represent Canada?" Dad asked.

Ron laughed. "Yes, our matches will be broadcast live—but you know what would be better? If you two would attend our games. Sis gave me enough for two tickets to Tokyo just before she left. It would be amazing if you two would cheer us on."

"Oh, Euodia. To think she did this for us!" Mom said in disbelief.

"Yeah, when I called her earlier today she was just as shocked as you guys when I told her we were qualified. She insisted on paying for the tickets for both of you to see me play. I can't wait to play for our country. It's going to be awesome!"

There was even more good news when Ron checked his email a week later. BC Electric had reviewed his interview and credentials and sent Ron a congratulatory email for being hired by the company.

Dear Mr. Lee,

We are happy to tell you that we have decided to move forward with accepting you as a business manager for our finance division. If you would like to take this position, please reply to this email, and we can schedule a date for you to start work.

Regards,

J. Horg

Printing out the email so he could show his parents, Ron smiled; there would be pizza in the house again knowing Mom, and he was glad he could honour his parents by achieving such a prestigious job.

"Dad! Mom! Guess wh—" Ron half ran, half jumped down the stairs, landing on the bottom with a thud. "Ouch!"

Mom looked up from her cooking and rolled her eyes; this son of hers would never learn to control his excitement —just like his father.

"Guess what? I got the job at BC Electric! I got the job!" Leaping up and down with excitement, he seemed more like a four-year-old getting candy.

Mom gave him a warm hug and patted his shoulder. "I'm happy for you, boy, but remember—getting a job also means you have to become more responsible."

Dad watched as his son bounced up and down, "Calm down, Ron! You're going to hit the ceiling at this rate. So what position was it that you got at BC Electric?"

"I'm accepted as a business assistant manager in the finance division. I'm just glad they overlooked my lack of experience. I can't believe I got the job!"

"Well, Son, you did graduate near the top of your class with honours, so I think you deserve it," Dad said. "Just be sure to work hard and don't slack off. If you don't put in enough effort, trust me, you'll be cut so fast you'll be wondering what happened."

"This good news deserves a celebration." Mom smiled as she picked up the phone and ordered pizza.

"Ron, you should probably tell Euodia, as well," Dad said. "She'll be quite excited for you to hear that you got the job."

Taking out his phone, Ron called his sister, eager to share the good news with her. "Hey, Euodia, guess what?"

"You're having pizza?" Euodia laughed at the surprised gasp in Ron's voice from her accurate guess.

"Yes, but it's not that. I got the job at BC Electric!"

"Congratulations! I knew you would make it. Your hard work is finally paying off, Ron." The sound of a bowl hitting the floor caused a distracted Euodia to clean up. "Chloe, we do not throw our food."

Ron chuckled at his niece's way of getting her mother's attention. "Alright, Sis, I'll let you get back to taking care of Chloe. Thanks. I just wanted to let you guys know."

"Good job, Ron. Work hard though, okay? We're all proud of you!"

Excited and anxious about starting his new job, Ron hung up and shook his head in disbelief, wondering what this next stage of his life would be like.

CHAPTER 12

ACCUSTOMING

Nearly two weeks later as Summer started with the promise of warmth, it wasn't the sound of birds chirping that woke Ron up. Instead, it was the shrilling alarm of his clock that signalled the start of the workday. From eight-thirty in the morning to four-thirty in the afternoon, Monday to Friday, Ron did his regular routine, managing the finances of the utility company.

Being part of a union of workers, he received a generous package of medical and dental benefits, RRSP matching, as well as sick leave if he needed it.

Finding time for badminton training was difficult as they prepared for the upcoming Sports Competition. It was not unusual for Ron to be away from home the entire day; if he wasn't at work, he was training for the badminton team.

During an ordinary Monday at work, Ron was in his cubicle, analyzing the costs of a new project assigned by his manager, Garret.

The buzz of the office was temporarily interrupted by a raspy cough from the other side of the office near the windows.

Walking over to his managing partner, Ron showed her his cost projections. "Hey, Rhonda, what do you think of these numbers? If the analysis is right, the cost of this project in total is roughly $40,000 dollars. Does that sound reasonable?"

"Hmm, that cost is quite high, but I believe the benefits will be higher given the improvements in the efficiency of delivering electricity to that district. But then again, it's not up to us to approve projects. We just calculate the cost and benefits. We'll leave the call for the head office."

Another cough sounded, this time in the back of the office near the washrooms.

"Alright, I'll get a start on the supply-chain cost for the procurement of equipment needed for this quarter," Ron said. "I probably won't finish, but I'll do what I can before going." He returned to his office chair and went back to crunching numbers.

A minute later, a head popped up over the cubicle wall; it was Anne, one of the office assistant staff. "I hear you play for the Canadian badminton team? So, are you guys going to Tokyo in the summer?" Her starstruck face looked as if she were talking to some celebrity actor.

Ron grinned, putting on a famous-actor smile. "You're right, Anne. Where'd you hear about that?"

"Oh, people talk and word gets around. We're happy for you and hope you'll do well!"

Sitting back down, she then stood back up and gave Ron a thumbs-up, leaving him confused by her awkward reaction.

Shaking his head, he busied himself with his work, ignoring the hum and buzz of an office workspace—people chatting and machines printing. Crunching the numbers, he was nowhere near finished, but his shift was about to end, so he decided that after a little longer, he would give what he managed to complete to the supervising manager when he punched out.

Getting up for a breather, he took his nearly empty coffee mug and went to the break room to refill. Seeing one last donut on the table, he was about to reach for it when Anne walked in and took the powdered donut, smiling at Ron. Hiding his disappointment, he filled his cup and walked back —sans donut, but with enough caffeine to get through the rest of the day.

With his shift ended and his coffee cup was empty, he logged out and cleaned up his space before filing his work for the supervising manager to check.

Looking outside, he saw that it was starting to drizzle, so he hurried and walked past the ever-emptying cubicles, trying to make it to his car before the rain turned heavy.

As fate would have it, he didn't make it, and by the time he was in his blue sports car, he was as wet as a cocker spaniel that was having its bath.

Grabbing a towel, he wiped down as best he could, and turned on the heat to dry his soaked hands. As the hot air circulated around the car, the windows began to fog up due to the moisture. Forced to turn on the defogging function, he waited what seemed like an eternity before the windows were clear enough to drive. Navigating through the relentless rain, he carefully slowed down, making sure to be safe while driving in such treacherous conditions.

Arriving at the gym, he sat in his car and devoured the vegan hamburger he had bought, watching the rain patter onto his windshield. As he closed his eyes, he imagined seeing Penny on their wedding day. She was wearing a beautiful wedding dress covered with pearls, with white flowers decorating the edges and train. As he reached out to take her hand, the whole vision disappeared, and he popped open his eyes as the sound of thunder woke him up.

Back to reality, he thought.

As he checked his watch, he saw that he still had ten minutes before training started, so he got his bags, rackets, and clothing, then dashed from the car to the building, trying to stay as dry as possible. After changing to his badminton attire, he joined the rest of his team training hard for the upcoming Sports Competition.

"Hey Steve, how are you?" he said to his teammate.

"Hey, man. My seasonal affective disorder has officially ended, but nothing like a mid-summer thunderstorm to put you on edge."

"Yeah, it's raining cats and dogs out there. I know, we can suggest to Coach to move our training centre to California, where it's nice and dry."

"I can imagine how that stunt would blow up in the news. 'Canadian badminton team trains in the USA—are they really, truly Canadian?'"

"Where's Xu?" Ron asked. "It's not like him to be late for practice." Ron looked around but couldn't find the iconic green shirt that his teammate friend liked to wear.

"Oh, the coach said he's sick or something. He's taking a few days off to recover—he probably just caught a cold or something."

Ron raised his eyebrows. "Catching a cold? You think he's playing hooky?"

"Nah, I know Xu. He's not one to fake something to get the day off. I had a call with him a day ago, and he sounded pretty bad. You know, with a raspy voice and cough."

"I'll give him a call later today, just to keep his spirits up, I guess. That's what my badminton buddies did for me when I got sick about three years ago. It really means a lot to get a call, you know," Ron said.

"Yeah, I've heard something about that, about you getting sick. What happened, man?"

Ron looked down at his feet, a flood of memories rushing to his head: him on the hospital bed, Mom and Dad, his badminton buddies calling, and Penny.

"You don't need to tell us if you don't feel okay with it, man. Don't worry, we'll understand," Steve said.

By now, several of the team had gathered around, all intrigued about Ron's past.

"It's fine, guys. About three years ago I had appendicitis, where my appendix got inflamed and I was put on a wait list for surgery. But due to a late diagnosis and the long waits in surgery, my appendix burst and I almost died from the infection. It was a miracle I actually survived, really. But I had my family and friends to care for me while I was sick."

And Penny tried to be there for me too. She died because of me, Ron thought.

He immediately changed the topic of conversation, not wanting to cry in front of all his teammates. After cracking a joke, he started warming up by running as fast as he could around the gym, leaving all his emotions and tears behind, not wanting to get ensnared by them as he had time and time again. It was just something he could not simply forget.

The rest of the team was bewildered but understood it was extremely painful for Ron, so they let the issue go. Soon, they too were warming up, ready for yet another day of training.

Watching the snow falling outside, Ron decided to call Xu to check up on his buddy.

"Hey Xu, it's me, Ron! How are you man? I heard you got a cold?" In the background Ron could hear some sort of machine compressing and decompressing, giving off the sound of air alternating between sucking in and gushing out.

"Hi—*shhhh*—Ron—*shhh*. Sorry I can't—*shhh*—talk—*shhh* —well. Hooked to—*shh*—a machine." The sound of air interrupted seemingly every other word as Xu gasped for breath between the breaks.

"Oh man, I'm sorry to hear you're sick, man. I've been in hospital before too, I know it feels horrible and alone. But hey, if you ever get lonely, give me a call whenever, and I'll be here to listen, okay? Don't give up. Never give up. There's always hope."

Hanging up the phone, Ron was wondering what had made Xu, a top-notch athlete, gasp for air like an old man. Little did he know that Canada, along with the world, was about to brace for the worsening of a widespread pandemic in the latter half of the approaching summer.

CHAPTER 13

CRISIS

"We have breaking news that the coronavirus, named COVID-19, has been infecting hundreds in Canada and possibly originated from Southeast Asia. Over twenty cases have been confirmed in BC alone over the last twenty-four hours, and cases are climbing exponentially once again after an initial decline in the hard-hit regions of Quebec, Ontario, Alberta, and British Columbia."

"Mom, are you seeing this? It's on the news, that new virus is spreading around BC fast. Nearly a hundred people have already died from the disease nation-wide!"

Ron's parents hurried to the TV, watching the same clips of nurses, doctors, and emergency workers wearing face masks, gowns, and shields that seemed to be what the prime-time news ever talked about every day.

Back at BC Electric, people were panicking, and it was absolute chaos. Anne and several other employees had tested positive, making other staff members wonder if they'd been exposed and infected as well. Everyone was required to wear a face mask, and the sight of an entire office of people, all trying to do their work in face coverings, looked more like a hospital than an office. The donuts that had been shared with everyone had been bought by a staff member who later tested positive for COVID-19, and anyone who took one of the donuts was asked to self-quarantine for fourteen days.

Rhonda walked up to Ron's cubicle, keeping her social distance of two metres. "Hey, Ron. You alright? You don't seem like yourself today. You're not sick, too, are you?"

"Nah, I was up all night talking with a friend. Actually, he's on our team for the Sports Competition, but right now he's on a ventilator with

COVID-19. I'm just really worried for him. He was fine one moment, then this."

"It's fine, Ron, just take your time. Don't push yourself and try to get those numbers done if you can, okay?

A slight cough from a window cubicle made everyone look fearfully in that direction. Rhonda shook her head, whispering quietly, "It's crazy here, man. People are freaked out. This world has gotten crazy."

"Yeah, nothing like a deadly infectious disease to make people fearful of death. No one thinks of their own death till it's staring them right in the face," Ron replied.

"What were you thinking about when you were hospitalized? Were you frightened at all?"

"Actually, I wasn't afraid of death, but I was severely depressed, and I feared that I'd be separated from my family, my friends, and Penny. Little did I know that even though I survived the ordeal, I would never see her again—I mean Penny, my girlfriend. Life has a cruel way of playing with our emotions."

"I'm sorry, Ron. I didn't mean to dig up your past." Embarrassed, Rhonda looked at her feet.

"All good, all good. It helps to remember what you've been through to remind yourself what you're capable of enduring and of how much you've been through."

"But doesn't it hurt? I mean, to uncover all those buried emotions all over again? Doesn't it hinder you from moving onward in life?"

"I disagree, Rhonda, the past shouldn't be forgotten. Rather, it should be a reminder of what we learned from the past, so that history doesn't repeat itself."

Rhonda's face showed she was thinking deeply about Ron's comment, as if she was remembering some past hurt that she'd experienced as well.

"Well, I better finish up here, Rhonda. Thanks for stopping by. I'll give you the results and total costs of November's project if I manage to finish them."

Giving Ron a salute, she walked back to her desk, carrying whatever private burdens she was bravely enduring, inspired by her coworker's view of coping with loss and pain.

Walking by the break room, Ron noticed that there were no more donuts, due to the office's fear of the unseen virus. Everyone had heard of how Anne had gotten sick after eating a donut bought by an infected staff member. Now snacks were avoided like the plague. People even sanitized their desks and chairs before using them.

Across the office, it was eerily quiet, as people, scared of being shunned for coughing, kept to themselves and worked as quietly as possible. Even the scanners and printers seem quieter, less noisy than the hum of constant printing barely a week before.

At badminton practice, all was silent as well, as Coach got everyone together for some disappointing news. "Everyone, I've got some bad news. It appears that due to the outbreak of coronavirus, the 2020 Sports Competition in Tokyo is postponed to the summer of 2021."

Moving his hands to quell the yells of protest and complaints from his players, he said, "Don't worry, guys.

We'll get our chance to play in 2021. We just need to be a bit patient, alright? That's all, everyone's dismissed."

"What do you think's going to happen to us? If Xu got sick, how likely is it that we'll get sick too? I mean, he's having trouble just breathing on his own, stuck on a ventilator machine ..." Steve said. He stared emotionless at the bench, not even bothering to look up.

Ron put his hand on his shoulder and relayed some wise advice he himself had learned from an older man. "Danger is either like a glass ceiling or a glass floor. If you're too afraid of it, it limits your capabilities like a ceiling, but if you treat it like a glass floor, you can reach new heights. But if you're not afraid of it enough to be careful, you may fall through the floor into ruin."

Ron smiled, watching Steve digest what he'd just said. Patting him on the back, Ron left the change room and got ready to go home, thankful that it had stopped raining. It seemed to have been raining for ages, so Ron gladly took the brief respite from the downpour.

Driving out of the parking lot, he decided to drop by his favourite restaurant for takeout to share with his parents. Ordering barbeque pork for Mom and himself, he also ordered a side dish of beef and *gie lan*, or Chinese broccoli, for his dad.

Looking at the nearly empty restaurant, he was amazed at how several weeks of a pandemic had changed things. There was plexiglass all around the counter, hand sanitizer at the entrance, physically distanced seating, and masks on all the servers and waiters. When his order came, he drove off back home, smelling the delicious Chinese cuisine waiting to be eaten, sitting in his backseat.

When he walked through the door, he called out, "Hello! I've brought dinner! Hello? Mom?" Looking around the kitchen and dining room, he saw no trace of his parents other than a small note on the dinner table.

Ron,

Will be back in a few minutes. Off to buy groceries.

Mom

Unpacking the dinner that he'd bought, he placed it on plates and kept them in the oven, to keep the food warm. Then he walked up to his room and made a call to Xu's mom, inquiring about his teammate's condition.

"How is he, Mrs. Chan? Is he still on the ventilator?"

"Hello, Ron, why don't you ask Xu himself? Here, Son, it's your friend Ron on the line."

"Hello, Ron?"

"Xu, you can talk normally now? That's awesome, man!"

"The doctors say I could be out by next week. It will be great to be able to go home. The hospital is excruciatingly boring, man."

"I know exactly what you mean, Xu. I was in the hospital three years ago as well. Nothing to do but eat, sleep, and repeat. Not to mention the joy of needles and taking pills."

"I wanted to thank you, Ron. You were right, there's always hope, and you were always there to listen and talk to me, as was my family. You were right."

"Just get well enough to play badminton, Xu. We need you for our men's doubles."

"I can't wait to get back into the game. My arm is itching to swing a racket."

"I felt the same way three years ago," Ron said, laughing. "You know what I missed the most? My own soft, comfy bed!"

"Ron, I have to ask. Has Coach Lucas, you know, found

someone to play in my place?" There was a bit of quavering in his newly found voice.

"You're asking if Coach replaced you? He has always had hope you would recover, so he hasn't found another player for men's doubles. Don't worry, we'll all be waiting for you to take your spot back. Alright, I hear my parents coming back home. Talk to you soon!"

Hanging up, Ron once again crashed down the stairs and again was chided by Mom for his recklessness. "Ron, if I got a dollar for every time you ran down those stairs, I'd be rich."

"Then I'll run down them even more to enrich my mother's coffers," he said, placing a swift peck on his mom's cheek.

"What about your poor, aging father, eh?" his dad asked.

"Speaking of what I have for my poor, aging father, here you go. Some beef and *gie lan* stir-fry!" After taking the food from the oven, Ron gingerly held on to the dish as he placed it on the dining table. Dad's eyes grew wide with eagerness. "And for Mom and me, barbeque pork, *char sui* with rice."

"You asked them for extra sweet soy sauce, didn't you, Ron?" said Mom.

Ron looked with mock horror at her accusation. "What, me? No! They gave me that much without me asking! Honest! Okay, okay, they already know I like extra soy sauce, so I didn't need to ask."

Mom tutted her son and laughed. "I don't even need to look to know what you're up to, Ron."

Dad whispered, "Honestly, she's got eyes on the back of her head."

Ron whispered back, "Not to mention the hearing of a night owl."

Mom turned around to face them. "What are you two murmuring about?"

"Err ... Nothing, just that we need to eat carefully to not upset our bowels," Ron said.

Mom looked suspiciously at her son before starting to cut up the pork for serving.

The pork was juicy, not so lean that it would be dry, but with just enough fat to keep the meat moist. Mom would always say to the butcher *boon fay, boon sao,* meaning half fat, half lean, and would never ask for too much of the sauce.

"How's the beef, Dad?" Ron asked.

"My brain is telling me it's absolutely delicious. I like it, I do. It's good." As if to prove his point, Dad finished his entire plate before Ron and Mom ate half of theirs. It was noted, though, that Mom always ate very slowly, savouring every morsel and rarely ever wasting any food.

"So how's your work?" Mom asked. "You have to be careful around your coworkers. Make sure you don't get too close to anyone who might be sick."

"I know, Mom. It's pretty secure. We all have temperature checks, and anyone with symptoms is sent home to isolate. I'm really safe, Mom. Don't worry. You're probably at more risk going to the grocery store. Have you guys tried online shopping for groceries?"

"Your mom wants to check everything before buying. There's always a chance to get a rotten apple when they pick your groceries for you," Dad said.

Shaking his head, Ron smiled at his parents' stubborn resistance to the change in technology and lifestyles. Earlier he had also asked if they wanted a smart home system, so they could lock the door remotely, control lights, and do other tasks. Dad didn't trust the technology, citing that it was "an overreliance on technology for safety, which creates a lack of experience in being prepared for life and its challenges."

Given his dad's reluctance to embrace technology, Ron was surprised that he was able to manage a business at all.

But somehow, his old ways of thinking didn't clash with the new technology used in his company.

Recently Dad had delegated most of his work to a senior manager, giving himself more time with the family to create memories that could be cherished for a lifetime.

Mom had been a stay-at-home mom for more than twenty years and had a successful side business of selling arts and crafts at farmer's markets. In addition, she managed the family garden, providing fresh fruit and vegetables during the spring and summer. She was also a master seamstress, repairing any tears or holes in the family's clothes and making new ones from ordinary fabric.

After turning on the TV, Ron and Dad watched the news as Mom worked on the dishes. Noticing Mom cleaning up, Ron decided to help clear up as well. They began a two-person system of washing and drying the dishes.

The news anchor on the TV reported, "British Columbia experiences steady growth in the number of new infections. It has been the third straight day of over ten cases, with two more people hospitalized."

"My teammate Xu's getting better in hospital," Ron said. "He might be released sometime next week. I talked with him on the phone, and he's doing much better than last week."

"I'd be careful around him, dear, even if he's asymptomatic. He still might be contagious."

"I will, Mom, don't worry. I've exceeded my decadal quota of hospital stays. Once every ten years is more than enough for a young lad like myself."

"There have been another outbreak in a care home in the Lower Mainland," the TV anchor continued. "Sadly, one senior was hospitalized and is in the intensive care unit. Seniors are more susceptible to the coronavirus, and it is more likely to be fatal among seniors."

Going back to his room, Ron lay on his bed, imagining

being in one of the movies posted on his ceiling. One of his favourite movies showcased a hero who somehow always lost his girlfriend—whether being kidnapped by a villain or befallen by some tragedy. The hero in another movie was in love but couldn't reveal his secret identity to his girlfriend.

Frustrated at the lack of a happy love-story ending in any of the movies, Ron imagined owning a house in the countryside, managing it with his wife, Penny, and taking care of their children. They would teach their children badminton, and Penny would practice physiotherapy while Ron continued his work at BC Electric. They would have campfires for marshmallows, s'mores, and bannock. Then they would all sleep in a tent under the stars, watching the glow of the fire grow dimmer and dimmer.

Then, suddenly everything was dark. Ron called for his wife and his kids, but there was no reply. It was just all darkness and silence.

He took a step forward and walked into a slough of what felt like mud that sucked his foot deeper and deeper. Slowly, his midriff went under the mud as well. By this time, Ron was panicking, and just as he took one last gasp and the ooze was flowing over his head, he bolted up and opened his eyes, realizing it was all a dream.

Checking his surroundings, he saw that indeed it was a dream. There was no mud at all, nor was there any evidence of Penny and their kids.

Pulling his covers over his body, he tried to remember the first part of the dream with his family, but like a waft of smoke, the moments were no longer in his memory. Instead of a house in the countryside, Ron saw only burned images, the searing light causing flashes of colour patterns in his mind's eye, even when his eyes were shut.

Then, suddenly, Penny and his kids were there, in his mind, but something was wrong. They acted like Ron wasn't even there. As Ron got closer to his family, they walked right past him, not recognizing him or even looking at him. Ron yelled at the top of his lungs, shouting that he was there, but to no avail. His yells were muffled and silent, as if his mouth was taped shut. Then, as his family started drifting away into the background, Ron noticed a man was amidst his family, but it wasn't himself. Shorter than Ron, with blond hair, broad shoulders, and long arms, he played with the kids and hugged Penny.

Anger turned to despair, and soon the entire scene in his mind shifted to darkness as he fell asleep, thankfully forgetting the gut-wrenching scenes when he woke up several hours later.

At breakfast, Dad said he wanted the family to visit the aquarium, but unfortunately for him, Mom and Ron didn't share his enthusiasm for fish. Dad had often told them of the many fish tanks he had as he was growing up. Over the years, from twenty gallons to a huge forty-gallon tank, it was apparent that Dad had nurtured a passion for fish from a very early age. He also told them that his favourite fish was the stick fish—a thin, ugly fish that resembled a twig. They were so hard to handle in a net, that he said staff at the pet store often needed to cut the net to free the twig-like creature from being entangled in it. The fishkeeping achievement he was most proud of was successfully breeding albino cory catfish. He told them the baby fry looked like red dots with tails, swimming around the substrate.

What amazed Ron the most was the sheer number of babies carried by female livebearer fish, like the black molly. One time, his dad and grandmother helped a molly give birth to roughly two hundred fry—although most were too weak to survive. They would be quarantined in a small baby tank to keep the fry safe from the larger fish—and even from their own parents, who would eat the defenceless babies if given a chance.

Dad also taught them that angelfish, on the other hand, would care for their eggs, picking out ones that had gone white with fungus and fanning them with their fins. But Dad never had any success breeding angelfish, even with the help of the parental fish. Guppies were very easy to breed, but Dad said they tended to interbreed with other livebearers, like mollies, platies, and swordfish.

Ron remembered being told how livebearers also tended to be very hard on the females, as males chased their mates day in and day out, often causing females to die of exhaustion.

One of the most fascinating fish that Dad owned lived longer than any fish he ever had. It was called a pleco and grew so big that it had trouble swimming around, even in the forty-gallon tank. It was an omnivore, feeding on algae and even dead fish carcasses. Sometimes it would feed on weakened fish, eating them while they lay dying.

One time, Grandpa helped eradicate an infestation of snails. He and Grandma boiled the gravel to kill off any snail eggs. The snails had decimated the plants in the aquarium and grown to be too numerous to handle.

Dad mentioned that Grandma often bought a plant called vallisneria, and the giant variety grew so large it would cover large sections of the top of the tank, like long streamers blowing in the water.

In fact, Grandpa one time built a forty-gallon tank for Dad, constructing the stand out of wood, painting it, and gluing the tank together with silicon. The cover for the top of the tank was made out of a plastic sign, with sections cut out to allow the cables and filters to poke through.

Shaking himself back to the present, Ron, along with Mom, conceded to go to the aquarium, carpooling in Ron's blue sports car. But it was clear from the sheer anxiety on Mom's face that she very much feared for her safety with her son at the wheel.

Once they were in the car, Dad put a comforting arm around her, letting her hand grip his in a death lock of fright. Both of them hung on for dear life as their son sped through the roads, utilizing the sports car's true horsepower.

Arriving at Stanley Park, they strangely enough found the parking lot empty, other than one or two vehicles.

Opening the door, Dad got out and pretended to kiss the ground, so grateful to be back on solid land.

"I'm sorry, Dad, but I think the aquarium's closed," Ron said. "There's no one here." Ron looked all around at the deserted parking lot and entrance.

Dad's face fell like he was a child who'd lost his ice cream, lamenting out loud, "We endured that crazy ride for nothing? Why are they closed? Perhaps they're opening later?" The note of optimism in his voice was clearly too hopeful.

"Sorry, Dad. Says here they're closed for the unforeseeable future due to the COVID-19 crisis. We'll come back next year, Dad, promise. Okay?"

Mom also hadn't fared too well with the ride. Holding her husband's hand, she was a bit nauseated, unused to both the lowness and speed of Ron's car. She much preferred her SUV, which had a higher viewpoint, compared to the ground-hugging bottom of the sports car.

"Ron," she said, "it's probably best if Dad and I take the bus home. I don't think I can survive another trip in that car of yours."

Ron's face showed his injured pride, as he thought he was an excellent driver. Penny had often enjoyed riding in his car. She often opened the window, letting the air brush her hand and blow through her hair.

"You two don't know good driving when you see it." Ron crossed his hands, hoping to prove his skill as a driver.

"I don't know who taught you to drive like that, but I assure it, it was not me or your mother." Dad crossed his hands together, challenging Ron comically.

Mom also crossed her hands, laying the blame without restraint. "I know we didn't teach him to drive like that, but who, I say who, suggested that he buy a sports car? Not to mention an expensive one!"

"Oh, so that's how it is?" Dad grinned mischievously. "Who, pray, fell for a guy driving a sports car thirty years ago and married him?"

"That was when I was young and naïve, dear, and without a care in the world. Now I've got to think of you, our kids, our grandkids—I mean, what would happen if one of us crashed? Our whole world would flip upside down! And I don't just mean that metaphorically! No, dear. My flirtatious years over sports cars are well over."

Dad smiled and gave Mom a kiss, understanding completely her concerns and worries. "We'd better get going on transit. It'll take a while to get back. So, Ron, get a start on dinner when you get back."

Mom agreed. "Yes, just grab the beef tenderloin from the freezer and let it thaw out. Don't forget. Otherwise, it'll be vegetables only for dinner. Also put three cups of rice in the rice cooker, but make sure you add enough water."

Ron nodded and hopped into his sports car, zooming around the corner. Mom glanced over at Dad with a look of confirmation. Indeed, he had a look of concern on his face as well.

"He was thinking of her, wasn't he?" Mom said.

"Yeah, that's what I thought too. I could tell by his face."

"He's still young. I'm sure we would've felt the same if we

lost either one of us. I'd say give him a few more years, then he might be ready to face what's next."

Dad simply shook his head. "It's just so hard seeing him like that. One moment he's fine and dandy, and the next moment he's depressed. There's no warning, no preventing it. They say a sad face is good for the heart, but I just want him to be happy."

"His loss has become part of his identity. He's somebody —the Ron we know now—because of what happened."

Chatting together, they walked to the nearest transit station, hand in hand, both concerned for the mental well-being of their son. The squirrels chatted among themselves as well, watching as the human couple left their forested territory, allowing them to gather nuts in safety once again.

Arriving home an hour later, Ron was just about to head upstairs when he remembered to take out the tenderloin. Opening the freezer, he found the beef as well as some pizza slices from their last celebration. He decided to reheat a slice in the microwave and take his snack upstairs. Biting into the saucy goodness, he juggled the hot morsel in his mouth to avoid burning his tongue before swallowing it whole. Taking another bite, he opened his laptop and checked for any emails among the spam that seemed to always fill his inbox.

Seeing an email from Dave, he opened it to see a picture of the whole gang, including Ben, waving their rackets. They were holding a banner up, that said, "Cheering for You in Tokyo 2021."

Ron smiled. They hadn't changed a bit in over three years. Still the same optimistic, cheerful, and energetic group they'd always been. He knew they cared about him, but with the new job and the training for the Sports Competition, he rarely had any spare time to spend with his buddies and chat. Perhaps after the competition, they could meet up again at the old gym and play a few games together for old time's sake and catch up with everyone.

Devouring the last of the pizza, he looked back to an email Penny sent years earlier:

> Ron,
>
> I know you wanted to watch *Mercy Spy*, but I think your father is right. I'm perfectly fine with watching *Maladie de la tête*. Trust me, it's not worth it to fight your parents. I've been there.
>
> See you at 1:00 PM.
>
> P.S. If I'm late, it's my dog's fault.

Scrolling back, he opened up another one:

> Ron,
>
> I'm so, so sorry I hit your head with my racket! I thought I had the space to smash. I'm so sorry! I'll be by later with some ice cream; what flavour do you want? Mint chocolate or vanilla?

Hearing his parents opening the front door, he quickly closed the laptop, composed himself, and walked silently down the stairs.

"My, my, is my son walking down the stairs civilly? What on earth happened to my reckless Ron?" Mom asked.

Ron smiled. His mom's sarcasm and humour were corny, but her efforts at trying to be funny were rare and far between. After checking the tenderloin Ron had taken out, Mom soaked it in some water to melt the centre of the meat some more before prepping it for cooking.

"What vegetables do you want, Mom? I'll help cook a bit. It's been a while since I cooked with you."

"As I recall last time, you cut yourself peeling potatoes."

Mom shook her head. "Prepare the English cucumber, carrots, and Brussels sprouts. But, please be careful this time. No injuries, please."

Mom then began work on the marinade, mixing dark soy sauce with honey, along with some rosemary. She tied the tenderloin in the ends and the middle and placed it into the oven with fingerling potato halves on the side.

Ron started peeling the carrots, then cut them into slices at an angle. He did the same with the cucumber while halving the Brussels sprouts one by one. Turning on the gas-powered stove, he poured a generous amount of vegetable oil, and once hot, put the carrots and Brussels sprouts in first, as they had to be cooked longer. Hearing the sizzling sound of oil, he knew it was hot enough to get a good charring sear on the vegetables. Covering the pan with a lid, he left it for a few minutes to cook.

In the meantime, opening the oven, Mom took the marinade and spread some over the half-cooked tenderloin, painting it on with a brush. She also coated the potatoes lightly with the same sauce. By this time, the smell was so delicious that Ron and his dad couldn't wait to start eating.

Mom looked at her son, with his face right up to the oven door, salivating and staring at the roast. "Ron, staring at the beef won't make it cook faster. Please, honey. What are you doing?" Mom turned around to see Dad walk up to the oven as well, sit next to Ron, and stare at the roast with him.

"Boys," Mom said with a sigh. She shook her head and went about setting out the cutlery. After about forty-five minutes, she finally took the roasted beef out of the oven, checked its temperature, and set it out to rest.

After sharpening her knife with the bottom edge of a bowl, she washed the blade and prepared to slice into the tenderloin. "Boys, back, back! Shoo. Sit at the table, boys. Stop getting in the way!"

Mom then sliced into the beef, and it was a perfect medium-rare, blushing pink in colour and smelling of the delicious, sweet soy-and-honey glaze. Collecting the juices and the drippings, Mom put them into a bowl, skimming some of the fat out, and placed it on the table for drizzling over when serving.

Setting the beef in the middle, Ron finished plating the vegetables while Dad spooned the rice into bowls. Ron looked over at Dad and saw him close his eyes for a second before joining in the meal with Ron and Mom. Ron started with the roasted fingerling potatoes, as his favourite food was potatoes, whether it was French fries, chips, roasted potatoes, or wedges. There was something about the starchy and filling nature of the spud that he always enjoyed.

The fingerlings this time were no exception. They were soft and had a hint of sweetness from the honey glaze.

Dad, on the other hand, went for the meat first, picking a slice of beef and chewing it with relish, complimenting Mother on another successful meal.

"Absolutely delicious dear. The honey makes it …"

Mom continued cutting the beef into small enough pieces so Ron and Dad could pick them up with chopsticks before she began eating. She used the *goong fai,* or serving chopsticks, to place several pieces of vegetables and meat into her bowl before putting it down and eating with her personal chopsticks. Just like Dad and Ron, she ate in a traditional manner, holding the bowl of rice with one hand and the chopsticks in the other. When it came to eating the rice, they brought the bowls to their mouths and *paa fan,* or rake rice—pushing the rice from the bowl into their mouths.

The Brussels sprouts were just soft enough, but not so soft to be mushy, and the carrots had a natural sweetness to them, being slightly charred.

Mom poured hot water into the rice pot, letting the leftover rice that had been baked on the outside of the pot soften up and be scraped off and eaten as *fan gew*, which had a hint of toasted rice flavour to it.

Pretty soon, everyone was full, while still pecking here and there at tiny morsels of meat or vegetable that lay hidden in the sauce. Dad let Mom and Ron have the leftover rice, and they slurped the hot water with the rice mixed in, sounding like vacuum cleaners sucking up some wet mess.

As Mom began clearing the table, Ron helped, starting to wash the dishes with dish soap. "Mom, should we fill up the sink with water?" he asked.

"It's okay, Ron, there aren't too many dishes. We can just quickly wash and rinse them all. It won't save much water anyway with so few."

Taking a grimy dish with a soapy hand, Ron almost lost it but caught it at the last second with his other hand, looking apologetically at Mom, who shook her head disapprovingly.

"Leave the acrobatics to the circus, please, Ron. I don't want to have to search for broken pieces of porcelain all over the kitchen. Remember the last time you broke the casserole dish? I'm still finding shards under the fridge even to this day!"

Ron smiled sheepishly, taking greater care to get a good hold on his dishes. Taking a greasy pot, he used his brute strength and a scouring pad and went to town with it, eventually revealing the shiny silver sheen of the pot underneath the grime.

Dad looked over and chuckled at his son's strong scrubbing. "You're going to scape a hole in that pot, the way you're scrubbing it."

"Just you wait, Dad. This pot will look like a mirror when I'm done with it. You'll see your own handsome reflection!"

"Dear, should we be worried our son is so die-hard and enthusiastic about washing the dishes?" Dad asked. He watched as Ron viciously attacked another greasy pot with a vengeance.

"I'd ask the same about my husband spending hours cleaning a fish tank!" Mom smirked. "Oh, don't think I haven't noticed you spending so much time on that aquarium of yours."

"Yes, dear, but I also spend many hours with you as well." Dad then winked at Mom, who shook her head, signalling that she was unamused.

"Don't try sweet-talking me, honey," she said, laughing. "What am I going to do with you? You're a lovesick puppy."

"Be honest, dear. You don't want me to beg like a dog, do you?"

Mom didn't comment and busied herself drying the rest of the dishes. Facing away from Ron and Dad, she hid a small smile. Dad was caring, protective, a provider, and sometimes absolutely hilarious—traits she was secretly glad he had.

Plopping down on the couch, Ron turned on the TV to check out the latest news happening in Vancouver and the world.

"Today, we spoke with organizers of the freedom rally, who said they planned to stage a protest at the art gallery tomorrow against the lockdown measures being implemented in BC," a reporter said. "They argue that the government has gone too far in violating people's freedom to not follow such procedures."

"Man, those people annoy me. All they talk about is freedom, equality, rights, and privilege," Ron said. "I mean, equality is only a façade. There are clear differences, and differences result in diverse versatility, different values, worth, honour, and glory."

Shocked and impressed with his son's interest in ethics and justice, Dad offered a suggestion. "Why don't you join the counterprotest then? You'd make a good debater, Son."

Walking into the room, Mom said, "Your father once debated, as well. It was one of the reasons I liked him. He would often stand up against injustice, and he could make a case for anything. His passion was undeterred by whatever he faced. Instead, the more challenging and dangerous, the more dedicated your father would be to fight it." Smiling at Dad, she rubbed his shoulders as they continued watching the news.

"Debating is crucial for determining importance, but you know what was the hardest debate I ever had?" Dad said. "It was to convince your mother to give me her hand in marriage. I came up with eleven points on why she should marry me."

Mom laughed and said, "Yes, I remember. And point five was my favourite. If I recall, it was that I should marry him because it would be an adventure, full of travelling, experiences, and excitement. And he did not disappoint, that's for sure."

"What about point one? That you should marry me because of my mediocre looks and shorter-than-average height." A sly look crossed Dad's face.

"Men all look ugly when they get old, and if you were too tall, I would have to tiptoe to kiss you."

Ron nodded. "That makes sense. Very logical of you, Mom. You know, Dad, I think I will go to that counter-protest. Maybe get in a few arguments against the protestors. Give them my two cents, eh?"

"I'd give them a dollar if I were you," Dad replied.

"A dollar? That would be overdoing it a bit, wouldn't it?" Mom was taking the imagery too literally.

"Not to me. I'd give them everything I got, just short of yelling like a madman," Dad told her.

"Just be careful, dear," Mom said to Ron. "You never know what these protestors are capable of doing when angered."

"Your mom's right. One time a fellow threatened me with a pocketknife over my views on immigration. Just know to stop debating when the time comes. There's a time and place for everything—even a time to back off."

"Alright, it's settled," Ron said. "I'll see what these protesters are made of before I challenge their privileged ideas." He went upstairs and began working on arguments supporting the act of listening to health experts and government authorities.

Typing away at the laptop, he found support using John Rawls's veil of ignorance, which states justice can be fair only if everyone decides laws and rules behind a veil or curtain, not knowing what position they would ultimately be in. In this theory, people will choose rules that are fair to disadvantaged people because there is a chance they'll be in that position when everyone is assigned a place.

Ron also found some information on Immanuel Kant's categorical imperative ideology, in which maxims that can't be universally tested should not be acted upon. Ron reasoned that if the protestors were morally correct in defying the government when it practiced overreaching powers, then all cases of government overreach should be resisted. But the protestors' idea failed the universalization test, as in times of warfare and severe emergencies, government must intervene. Therefore, the protestors' obligation to rebel was contradictory and irrational, being not applicable in all plausible cases.

Feeling quite accomplished in his arguments, Ron took a swig out of his day-old coffee and pulled a face. He took the cold, spoiled liquid to the kitchen to dump it out. Quickly rinsing the cup, he set up the coffee machine to make himself a new cup, creating an aroma of the breakfast-blend coffee as it slowly dripped into his waiting mug. Getting sugar from the cupboard and some milk out of the fridge, he added them to the coffee, making the liquid a light-brown colour. Tasting it, he quickly glanced at Mom, who was preoccupied with the TV, and sneakily added another two tablespoons of sugar. Finally, he tasted it and approved of its sweetness.

"Ron, you put extra sugar in your coffee, didn't you?" Mom didn't even turn her head to watch her son's surprised, yet guilty, look.

Dad turned and pointed at the back of his head, signalling Mom could see from both front and back. When Mom turned to see what her husband was doing, he became suddenly preoccupied.

Ron laughed while watching his dad trying to keep out of trouble. His parents were meant for each other—one funny, one sarcastic, one quick-witted, one thoughtful. But most importantly, both were hardworking and committed to one another. Ron had heard of some of his friends in school who had parents break up, wreaking havoc with their family life.

Looking at a family portrait in the hallway, a sudden flash brought back a flood of memories. Ron thought for a second that he saw Penny and himself in the picture, with their two children. But just as fast as lightning, the image disappeared, and he returned to reality.

Then he remembered his dream—the blond, fair-skinned man hugging Penny and her children. Thinking carefully about the dream, he realized that one of his children had blond hair, while Penny and Ron both had jet-black hair. Troubled by the confusing dream, he went back to working on his arguments for the next day's counterprotest.

The next morning, after several hours of studying his arguments, Ron drove his sports car through the strangely clear highways of Surrey. He decided to stop by his favourite dim sum shop for lunch. After parking the car in the nearly empty parking lot, he got out and saw the sign on the front door:

> Dear guests and patrons,
>
> Due to restrictions and regulations because of COVID-19, we have decided to close until further notice. We apologize for the inconvenience and we look forward to seeing you dine in with us again.
>
> FF Chinese Restaurant

Disappointed with the closure, Ron checked his watch. There was enough time for another option. He decided to go to a fried chicken shop, where he ordered a five-piece chicken-and-fries combo.

Being of a stocky and big build, Ron was able to clear the combo meal in record time, until only bones and leftover ketchup were left on his plate.

Driving through the rest of North Surrey, Burnaby, and Vancouver, Ron noted the lack of traffic. It was a Saturday afternoon in what would usually be a gridlocked city full of cars, buses, and trucks. Ron arrived at the art gallery thirty minutes later, parking quite a distance away so as not to endanger his vehicle. Grabbing his counterprotest sign, he headed towards the two large groups facing off against each other. When he arrived, he listened to the two leaders arguing toe to toe.

"I have a charter right not to wear a mask and to keep socializing in whatever gathering I want. We aren't in a crisis, there's no pandemic, and everything scary about COVID-19 is fake news!" the protest leader said.

"What's it going to take for you guys to listen to the health officials?" the other replied. "One hundred deaths? Two hundred? What will you say to those whose parents and grandparents are stuck in death traps, those care homes facing the nearly unstoppable spread of the virus? Your vigilante beliefs and actions are reckless and irresponsible, as you are only about yourselves and not those who stand to lose the most due to the coronavirus."

"The facts speak for themselves. There are only a hundred or so patients in the hospital right now and in total only two hundred and fifty deaths in BC since the start of the year. That's not a pandemic. There's no justification for shutting down the economy and using authoritarian-style tactics to control everyone."

"You're wrong. The reason the numbers are so low is that we have stringent laws in place right now. If we reopen the economy fully and let people do what they want, the number of deaths could be in the thousands. Will it take a thousand deaths before you realize the severity of this pandemic?"

Another protester chimed in. "Who's going to pay the cost of the millions of jobs lost due to the shutdowns? Who will pay for parents who have to quit their jobs to look after their children because schools are closed?"

The leader of the counterprotest wasn't unnerved at all but was prepared for such a question. "Those jobs will come back in the long run, but for now, the cost of letting people die due to this virus is way higher than the cost of temporarily high unemployment. People may lose their jobs, but they'll be safe, and new jobs will come later as we recover."

Pretty soon, both sides were getting more and more scrappy, and police were called in to maintain the peace. Some protesters threw stones at their opponents, while both sides hurled insults, turning the protest into a contest of who had the vilest language.

Ron left soon after, as there wasn't much debating going on and people were just acting on their emotions rather than out of reason and thoughtfulness. Putting away his Listen to Advice sign, he drove off, away from the commotion, leaving the mockers and brawlers to fight it out.

While he was driving home, a call from Dad came in on the Bluetooth. He was wondering how the debate was going. "How was it, Son? Did you manage to convince some naysayers? I should have gone with you. I wouldn't have minded scrapping it out a few more times."

"You didn't miss anything, Dad. It was a joke. People didn't go to debate; they just wanted a reason to get off work or chuck stuff at the police. No reasoning at all whatsoever. Completely pathetic. But I did manage to hear the counter-protestor leader speak, and he seemed very informed and decent. I liked several of his points against protesting the government's policies, and I think it makes sense."

"Oh, when I protested the selling off of agricultural land in the ALR, I led the charge against the counterprotesters who wanted to develop it. You have to make simple yet important points to argue efficiently. Too long, and they won't let you speak. Too simplistic, and it won't matter to them. It has to be both short and poignant, important but digestible."

"Like dough bits, tiny donuts but packing a punch of flavour!"

Dad pondered over his son's words, wondering where on earth his reference to food came from. "Err, yeah, like, dough bits. But the important thing is that you made your voice heard. They say evil men flourish when good men do nothing. Having a cause to fight for is crucial to getting through those hard parts of life. Under extreme pressure is when your real cares, wants, and core values will be revealed."

As he chewed on his father's advice, Ron's stomach suddenly growled and he realized that he hadn't eaten anything since lunch. "Dad, do you and Mom want something to eat later? I can drop by the butcher shop and grocery store. I'm getting a craving for barbeque roast duck and noodles. I'll grab dessert as well; how many Portuguese egg tarts do you want? A half dozen?"

"Now that you mention it, I'm also craving duck and noodles." Dad turned away from the phone and called out, "Mom, what do you think? Are you craving duck and noodles as well?" He laughed and returned to the phone. "Your mom says yes. Oh, and I'll take half a dozen Ports."

"I'll be home in about an hour, then. Talk to you guys later."

Arriving at the supermarket, Ron headed for the butcher stand, where rows of barbeque pork were hanging, dripping with oil. On another hanger, half a roast pig was dangling.

He indicated to the butcher that he wanted the roast duck and didn't want it cut up. With the meat secured, Ron then picked up three packs of *lai fun*, a type of Chinese rice and tapioca noodle. After picking up a Chinese vegetable called *yui choi*, as well as some broth, the last item he got was the egg tarts, twelve in total and still warm from the oven.

Lining up at one of the cash registers, Ron piled the luncheon items onto the belt and by chance happened to look up at the manager's desk. What Ron saw made his jaw drop.

There at the desk was Michelle, his girlfriend from over seven years earlier. Not wanting her to spot him, he slouched over and turned his face, which by now was rosy-pink with embarrassment.

Hiding behind the candy bars, he wished the cashier would scan everything faster, as he couldn't wait to leave the awkward situation.

Ron had broken up with Michelle with a text message, as he was too afraid to tell her directly. After that, Michelle never texted him back despite Ron's assurance they could stay friends.

She had a dominating character, not trusting him and

wanting to do things her way always. They had dated for only about a month before he realized they were not a good fit as a couple.

Quickly paying the cashier, Ron took his groceries and quickly walked the whole distance from the cashier stands to the entrance before breathing a sigh of relief at not being caught by his ex.

Relaxing his shoulders, he suddenly felt a tap on them. Turning around, he found himself staring point-blank at Michelle, her eyes piercing his soul like a knife.

"Uh … Hi, Michelle. I didn't, uh, know you worked … um … Here." The awkwardness of the situation would have made a frog blush. "Well … It was, uh, nice meeting you again. I'll be going—"

"Say it to me directly. C'mon, say it. Tell me why you broke up with me." She put her hands on her hips, like she was an agent interrogating a pitiful prisoner.

Ron wanted to crawl under a rock and stay there forever. "I, uh, honestly didn't like not being listened to. You were just … uh. Too headstrong? I'm sorry, it's just that I couldn't find room for you in my heart."

Unfortunately, there were no rocks to hide under, but he thought perhaps the sewer would do. "I'd better get going, my parents are waiting for their dinner."

Trying his best to put on a fake smile and waving awkwardly, he walked away from what seemed like the most uncomfortable situation one could be in. Walking to his sports car, he felt Michelle's eyes were still stabbing into his head, her glare locked onto him like a sniper. Shaking it off in the car, he pulled out and was glad to leave that awkward encounter.

By the time he got home, the duck was cold and Mom had to warm it up in the oven. She sliced the skin off the duck and cooked the broth over the stove. The noodles were cooked separately in another pot, and the vegetables were sautéed in a pan with oil and salt.

Ron poured boiling broth into three large bowls while Mom divided up the noodles into each of them. Taking the duck from the oven, she placed the meat on one side and the skin on the other for each bowl. Lastly, several stalks of *yui choi* were placed on each side as well.

Picking a small feather root from a skin, Ron dove head-first into the meat, enjoying the duck's savoury flavour.

Mom, on the other hand, nibbled at the vegetables and used a spoon to taste the broth. The saltiness of the duck meat contrasted against the natural sweetness of the *yui choi*. The crispy, roasted taste of the duck skin was second to none, and the broth was extremely delicious. The noodles were like a treasure hunt, as more and more of them were eaten. The rest were hidden like buried treasure in the broth.

Soon Mom, Dad, and Ron were hunting for morsels, finally resigning to slurping the golden-coloured soup. Ron took out the egg tarts and gave himself and Mom three regular tarts each while Dad got six Portuguese tarts. Dad bolted down his six tarts like he was in a famine, while Mom nibbled hers ever so slowly. Taking advantage of Mom looking the other way, Dad was able to steal an egg tart from under her nose while she daintily ate her first tart.

Looking down at her remaining tarts, Mom sighed. "Honey, you could have at least asked."

"Dear, I know you so well that I didn't need to ask. I knew you wouldn't resist such a charming husband's request for an egg tart." Dad gave Mom the most innocent of looks, which would have charmed a bird out of a tree.

Mom rolled her eyes. Looking at her son, she knew something was wrong. "Ron, something's bothering you. What is it?"

Surprised at having been detected, he dropped his head in

resignation. "I saw Michelle today while getting the groceries. She demanded I tell her directly why I broke up with her."

Dad was surprised. "Wow, that girl doesn't mince words. But aren't you glad I told you she's not your type? A nagging wife is very undesirable."

Ron smiled at his dad, who always thought he was a master of romance, always advising on Ron's dating relationships. Taking the bowls and chopsticks, Mom and Dad got up and put them in the sink to be rinsed as Ron wiped down the table with a rag. Using the last bit of dish soap, he shook the container, trying to finish the rest. "Mom, we're out of the soap. Do you have more in storage?"

"Yes, it's under the sink, next to the buckets."

Taking out a new bottle, Ron marvelled at the bright, unnatural colour of the soap, wondering how on earth they made the liquid as bright as it was. Mom put on gloves as she prepared to rinse the dishes after Ron washed them with soap. Her hands suffered from eczema, and it seemed the more she washed her hands, the drier they became. Hence the need for gloves.

Looking at the bottle of soap, Ron saw the duckling on the label covered with oil. "Mom, do you think they purposely put oil on that duck to show how effective the soap is?"

"Dear, if you're looking for a moral, conspiracy, or ethics debate, please ask your dad. I will stay neutral in all matters. Absolutely no comment from your dear old mother."

"Your mother is like Switzerland. Too frightened to take a side," Dad said, laughing.

Mom gave a slight look of annoyance at the insult. "If you don't pick a side, you don't get hurt, dear."

"Nonsense, if you don't pick a side, you'll never win. You

can't be neutral all the time. Lukewarm water is neither cold nor hot. It's useless."

"Pardon me, but neutrality is like baking, not water. If you undercook or overcook bread, it's useless. You have to find the middle, where it's perfectly cooked."

"No, no, dear," Dad said. "It's like baking a roast. If you use too low a temperature, it won't bake. The quickest way to cook it is to turn the heat up to the max."

Mom frowned at all the points made against her. Focusing on rinsing the dishes, she didn't notice Dad coming behind her. He gave her a warm, bear-like hug, kissing the back of her head.

"My dear Switzerland, come to my side, and we'll fight for victory together," Dad said.

Ron admired how quickly Dad managed to patch up after their heated debate. Pretty soon, Mom was back in a good mood and both were chattering together, smiling, and laughing.

Ron smiled and quietly snuck back upstairs to his room, leaving the two lovebirds in the kitchen.

Taking out his wallet, he touched the pocket photos one by one, seeing how happy Penny had been, both of them making goofy faces. He remembered that afternoon when they took those photos. It was at a shopping mall kiosk, where they'd crammed in together and paid a dollar; watching the camera flash three times. Ron had complained that the flash was too bright, blinding him. Penny had laughed at him, calling him a big baby.

After they retrieved the photos, they'd headed over to the cinnamon bun shop, lured by the delicious aroma of cooking sticky buns. Tearing into the gooey, sweet pastry, they laughed at how messy they both looked: fingers sticky with sugar and mouths splattered with cinnamon.

They washed up, then they went to the candy store on the

second floor. Penny bought some candy that looked like metal beads—more metallic than sugary—while Ron chose soda and block candies, paying for both his and Penny's share. Sitting by the fountain, they popped candy into their mouths as they watched the water shoot up in a display of patterns, awing them with the rhythm of the water and the LED display lights.

Before they headed back home, Ron decided to get a souvenir for Dad and Mom, opting for some fake plastic sushi rolls—knowing Dad liked to eat sushi.

Riding home, they discussed whether it was good to buy an electric vehicle and whether the environmental movement was as important as it seemed.

Ron hesitated to give full support for buying an electric vehicle, noting that he liked the raw power and speed of a sports car's gas engine.

Penny disagreed and thought the savings on gas and the pollution-less aspects were truly important ones to consider.

But they both agreed that safety was a big issue, especially if they started a family. They both also believed that an SUV would be best for accommodating the needs of a growing family.

Ron thought fossil fuels would better be used during abnormally cold-weather phenomena, such as The Little Ice Age that hit Europe hundreds of years before.

Penny asserted that technology had a key role in helping countries be more ecologically responsible and that countries that invested in green, renewable technology would benefit the most in the long run.

Amazed at the well-educated answers Penny gave, Ron enjoyed talking with her and gaining a better understanding of her values, morals, and heart.

Not only was she a good debater but Penny was also a top-notch student, working on a kinesiology degree and hoping to become a fitness trainer or physiotherapist. She was in a co-op, studying for half the week and working as a trainee for the other half. Ron had even let her practice her muscle massaging techniques on him, and he always strongly stated how awesome and relaxing it felt.

But offering himself as a test subject also came with risks, as Penny had once accidentally pinched a nerve on his shoulder, causing his muscles to tense up for the entire day. She apologized, being extremely embarrassed. But Ron shrugged it off and reassured her that it was fine and just slightly bothersome even though it felt like his arm was frozen.

Standing in his room, deep in memory, Ron rotated his shoulders, missing Penny's physiotherapy—especially after a tiring day of work and badminton. What he wouldn't have given to have her massage his back again.

Walking over to his desk, Ron checked for emails on his laptop, finding the usual spam from social media notifications and the latest deal from his bank. He never really took the offers from the junk mail, except for one occasion when a store was offering a free phone and gift card for five hundred dollars with the agreement to a two-year term on the phone. Other than that, most of the spam went straight from the inbox into the trash, without a second thought or consideration. One particular email in his social media category, though, caught his eye:

Do you know Michelle Zia?

Supervising Manager at Z&P Grocery Stores

It was another suggested acquaintance for his networking app, but this time it was his ex-girlfriend who was in question.

He decided to delete the message and moved it to the trash to avoid any awkward consequences. Ron thought back to how they'd endured a naïve relationship seven years earlier, when Ron didn't quite know what to look for in a girl or how to communicate what he wanted.

Michelle had the looks and charm but was far too dominant for Ron, who was more traditional and orthodox. He was looking for a well-mannered, submissive girl.

After four months of casual small talk and gift-giving, he finally got the courage and asked her out to see a movie. It was then Ron learned Michelle wanted to be a police officer and commandeered much of the conversation between them. Not wanting to make the situation embarrassing and awkward, he decided to explain the reason for breaking up in a text, saying how he wanted to stay friends but nothing more due to incompatibility. He never got a text back from her, and he assumed she didn't wish to see him anymore. This troubled Ron, as he figured he may have been too blunt.

After washing up, he got ready for bed, kicking off his socks and lying on the bed minus the pillow. He found that without the pillow, his back pain disappeared, hence he now always slept on the bed without it. As he drifted off to slumber, a vexing, troublesome thought began building in his mind.

In his mind's eye, he again saw Penny with two children, and they looked up and greeted him. Ron smiled, but something wasn't right. He noticed they were greeting someone to his left, not him.

Then a short blond man walked past Ron and picked up one of the kids. Penny held his hand, and the other child followed suit. Ron tried shouting to Penny to come to him, but when he opened his mouth, nothing came out. His voice was muted. In desperation, he tried running towards her, but she, the man, and the children all were moving farther and farther away the more he ran, until they disappeared into the horizon.

Then darkness began shrouding Ron, engulfing his body and finally his face, suffocating him in the cloud. Then, as he was getting lost in the chaos, he heard Penny's voice: "It all depends on whether you resent or are content with what you have. Fairness is a decision. It is a choice we all can make. It is a choice ... It is a choice ... It is a choice."

As he was about to give up all hope of escaping the darkness, it suddenly spiralled away, just as fast as it had come. When he dared to open his eyes, he was in a playground, somewhere that seemed vaguely familiar in his mind. Indeed, it was his old playground from childhood, where he would often bike to and play with his friends.

Then he recognized his father—younger and happier and pushing a much-younger Ron on the swings.

They looked so content, oblivious about the worries of life, just enjoying the moment, one minute at a time. Then, in a gutsy manner, the young Ron decided to jump from the swing and onto the gravel on the ground. But he mistimed it and landed hard, scraping both his knees. Dad immediately went to help, but suddenly Mom appeared, caressing Ron and wiping his wounds with some tissue that she always kept with her.

Dad then carried Ron in his arms, holding him carefully, while Mom rushed to get the car door open. As they drove off into the distance, Ron noticed the drops of blood, trailing across the sidewalk to where he'd landed on the ground, staining the innocence of the once-clean playground.

Soon after, the playground scene faded out of view and a new scene emerged, this time when Dad had convinced the whole family to join a summer camp.

During the camp, Ron was in the lecture room, tuning out the speaker's monotonous, droning talk. The afternoon was better, as they enjoyed a delicious brunch and played some sports in their free time.

When it was time to play badminton, Ron hoped to show everyone his skill, but he noticed a player who was slightly handicapped. He realized that the rest of the players didn't want to partner with this individual. So Ron paired up with his disabled friend and waited in line to play. Unsurprisingly, they did horrible as a team, but Ron felt it had been the right thing to put aside fun and glory in exchange for mercy, compassion, and inclusivity.

As Ron's dream continued, his memory of the camp and his imagination began to blur, and reality became harder and harder to decipher. He was walking along a path in the camp one moment, and the next he was sucked into a vortex of blue light. While he continued to descend to the pit, he kept hearing the same words over and over from family, friends, and even Penny:

It's your fault.

Dear, she died because of you.

You're responsible, Ron

It's all your fault. It's all your fault.

It's all your fault!

Waking up, he was drenched in a cold sweat. As the nightmare subsided, he lay back down, opening his eyes every few seconds to make sure he didn't end up in another nightmare, afraid to completely fall asleep.

After several hours of tossing and turning, he heard the chirping of birds and smelled the aromatic coffee being brewed downstairs. Ron slowly walked down the stairs, holding on to the railing.

"My, my! Did you age a decade, Ron? You're holding on to that railing like an old man!" Mom exclaimed.

Hearing that comment, Dad politely coughed. "And pray,

dear, what's wrong with an old man?" he asked. He raised his eyebrows so high they could've reached the sky.

Both of them stopped the humour when they detected that something with Ron wasn't right. Dad stood up and took his hand. "Son, is there something wrong? What happened?"

"Mom. Was it … Was it my fault that Penny … That she died?" Tears began to well up in Ron's eyes. "She died because she wanted to see me?"

Exchanging glances with one another, Mom and Dad hugged Ron tightly, reassuring him, and Mom said he did nothing wrong. "Ron, no one could have stopped that car from crashing into Penny. It's not your fault, Son."

"But … But, if I hadn't been so sick, she wouldn't have driven to see me … And … And she'd be alive." It was too much; Ron broke down in tears and hugged Mom and Dad ever more tightly.

"Ron, we can't go back and imagine what if this or what if that happened. You'd be so full of regrets that you'd sabotage your success," Dad said. "You can't move forward unless you stop stepping on the brake pedal of looking back. Since it's impossible to move back in time, you can step on the gas and move on with your life, or you can hold on to the brake, stopping and dawdling, thinking of what might have been. No matter how hard you try, Ron, you can't go back and save her."

"I try moving on, Dad, but I keep getting these … These flashbacks, memories, and dreams. They keep coming up every once in a while, and it makes no sense at all. And … And every time I remember or see something, it reopens the wound of losing her. And I just can't heal … Nothing's the same anymore."

"Ron, not a day passes by that I don't think of Daniel," Dad said. "But I keep those good memories stashed away in my brain and don't get bogged down with guilt, anger, or grumblings. You probably won't forget about Penny, but what I'm saying is, don't let it incapacitate you. Remember her, feel sad or happy, then move on to the next moment in life. There's a quote from some wise person. 'The death of a beloved is like an amputation' because while you may heal, you're never the same. As for your dreams, don't let them trouble you too much. But keep a record of what they're about. If they keep repeating, there may be a reason for it."

After comforting his son with those words, Dad patted Ron on the back, and Mom handed him another tissue before turning back to finish cooking breakfast. Dad got up and poured a cup of coffee. "Here, Ron, have a cup of joe. It'll help you feel better," he said.

"Thanks, that would be great, Dad. Milk and lots of sugar, please." Ron looked over at Mom, who usually chided his sugar tooth, but this time she let him be.

Mom placed several pieces of buttered toast on everyone's plate, and Ron proceeded to put peanut butter on them. Opting for the crunchy peanut butter—as it tasted better than the smooth ones—he piled it on thick and finished it off with slices of banana. Still thinking of Penny's death and having it weigh heavily on his mind, he tried to focus on eating.

Dad looked at the toast and recalled a memory. "You know, Ron, until I left home when I was thirty, I ate peanut butter toast and oatmeal almost every day. Not to mention we never ate butter or margarine and used only very little sugar or salt because of your health-conscious grandma."

"Are you serious, Dad? I couldn't imagine not having butter or margarine—not to mention ice cream, chocolate, coffee, chips. They say butter makes everything better."

"Well, since you train and work out so much, it's okay that you eat a little unhealthy. It balances out. But it's ultimately each person's own choice whether to eat junk food or healthy food. Food can make people happy, yet health can make people happy as well. It all depends on which is more important to each person and how they want to balance the two. Your mother values healthier food, while I, on the other hand, like satisfying junk food once in a while. She completes me, and it's like we're in perfect balance."

"But Penny and I were so like-minded. We both worked out, we both thought a lot about nutrition, we both liked badminton, and we both liked to be funny."

"Couples with similar values and beliefs get along much better than those with opposing traits; they virtually agree almost all the time. But the pitfall is that they both suffer the same weaknesses and are prone to falling in those weak areas. But if you have a wife who counterbalances your weaknesses, like how your mom covers me, you're less likely to fall as a team. Where I'm weak, she's strong, and where she's weak, I'm strong. We average out to be more stable. So, it's up to you, whether you want a more dynamic, adventurous, volatile relationship or a less exciting but steadier one."

Ron went back to tackling his breakfast, contemplating what Dad said while chewing morsels of toast and eggs. When he cut the yoke of the sunny-side-up egg, the liquid gold flowed out, and he wiped it up with his toast. Picking up a strip of bacon, he crunched it bite by bite, savouring the saltiness of the meat.

Dad once again used nearly a quarter of the bottle of ketchup on his omelet and innocently cut it up into bite-size pieces. Mom opted for sausage links and relished the seasoned meat with a slight hint of peppercorn and spices.

Dad's plate also had his favourite food—potatoes—as he was eating both hash browns and tater tots. He often commented that he could live on potatoes alone. His favourite dish when he was a child was pork and potatoes, made by Grandma. Ron's favourite snack, on the other hand, was mint chocolate ice cream and mint chocolate candies.

Like his son, Dad had a liking for chocolate candies, and Grandma used to give him little sweets as a sort of bribe to make sure he behaved. Of course, if it didn't work, there was always the old-fashioned way of disciplining: by the feather duster or stitch.

Having grown up being disciplined for wrongdoings when he was a child, Dad also made sure to discipline Ron, but Dad was very careful to make it purposeful, meaningful, and not arbitrary, excessive, or abusive.

Ron had once stolen candy from the grocery store bulk section. Dad made him apologize to the store clerk, then they drove all the way home in complete silence. By then, Ron knew what was coming. When they got home, Dad took hold of him and, using his hand, spanked Ron several times on his behind until Ron started to cry. Then Dad explained why he was getting spanked and why he shouldn't steal again. But most importantly, Dad explained that he was disciplining him because he and Mom both cared about him a lot.

Euodia was disciplined much more by far, as she was constantly caught bullying Ron or being abusive. But even with the discipline, she was like a whirlwind—hard to control and prone to destructive behaviour.

One Halloween, Euodia convinced Ron to throw rotten eggs at a neighbour's house. When Dad found out, he was calm but serious about what he wanted to teach his children. They both got punished by having their hands hit with a stitch. Dad explained why they deserved it and made them promise not to ever do that again. In the end, with many tears being shed, the family hugged in reconciliation.

Of course, when Ron grew older, he smartened up and learned to behave, leaving behind his childhood shenanigans.

Physical discipline was eventually phased out and replaced with verbal lecturing.

Not only were Ron and Euodia taught to avoid bad behaviour, but Dad also taught them to be proactive in helping each other, such as helping Mom clear up the dishes after every dinner.

This morning was no exception, and Ron took the breakfast plates and utensils to be soaked in the sink. Again, he took the soapy side and left Mom with the job of drying the dishes. Dad took a rag and started wiping the already clean table, scrubbing at nearly imaginary specks of dust and grit.

Heading to work, Ron had a full belly and a mind nearly full of advice and information from his breakfast conversation.

Finding a parking spot at work close to the entrance, he noticed several small smart cars that were rented on demand. But it was strange to see so many, as most of the office staff drove their own cars. Chancing a glance at one of the cars, he noticed a strange briefcase on the passenger side —one that seemed too large for business, like the ones used to carry large tools, sports rackets, or guitars.

Walking inside, he felt the blast of air conditioning blow past his face. Shaking off a shiver, he greeted the security guard and walked in. "Morning, Clyde!" he said. Walking over to his cubicle, he looked over and saw a familiar face. "Hey, Rhonda, how's it going? I hear you got engaged! Congratulations!" he said.

"Well, it was supposed to be a surprise, but apparently someone can't keep a secret." As she said that, she looked towards the far cubicle, where Wendy worked.

"You on, the other hand … Well, thank you for not spilling the beans on my secrets. You know, about me and my parents. You're a good friend, Ron. It's pretty hard to deal with people looking down on you and judging too."

Ron recalled listening to Rhonda's story about how she fought with her parents till the point where she stormed out of the house, vowing never to return.

"Did I hear someone mention beans? Someone left a jar of pickled kidney beans in the break room. Help yourselves!" said John as he passed. After he looked away, Rhonda made a silent puking gesture, indicating the toxicity of the apparent free snack.

Ron gave her a thumbs-up in acknowledgement, walked to his cubicle, and picked up the paperwork he needed to start on.

When he sat down, as always, he felt like he was being squeezed into the tiniest chair. And it was getting worse, as he'd gotten bigger after getting back to regular workouts at the gym.

Writing a quick note to the supervising manager above him, he requested a larger office chair, preferably without armrests. They tended to be unused anyways, taking up valuable arm space.

Logging into his computer, Ron reviewed all his work emails and found out that Anne, one of their coworkers, had succumbed to her COVID-19 infection.

The company was starting a fundraiser to help her parents take care of her only child—a girl who was only four years old. Ron shook his head in disbelief. It seemed like only yesterday she was talking to him about the Sports Competition.

He thanked his lucky stars that he hadn't taken the donut that day—the donut that Anne took that had been bought by a man with COVID-19.

Scrolling through the rest of the emails, he came across a new procedural checklist the company had sent:

> Dear employees, as we tackle this unprecedented time of worldwide pandemic, we are enforcing strict measures to keep all our office staff safe and healthy. Please adhere to the following rules:
>
> 1. Please wash your hands frequently, cough into your elbow, and wear a mask.
>
> 2. No gatherings of over 3 people in the offices.
>
> 3. No more sharing of open or unsealed food in the break room.
>
> 4. Keep at least 2 metres apart from other employees.

Shutting his eyes, Ron imagined back to the days before COVID-19, before people cringed at every single cough, before sharing was a sin, before hugs were forbidden. He snapped open his eyes at a polite cough beside him.

"Ahem, did I catch you at a bad time, Ron? You're not the one to daydream. Quite odd, quite odd indeed, eh?"

Ron quickly offered an apology to his supervising manager. "Sorry, Garret, I just needed a pause after reading all the emails about COVID-19. It's rather depressing and unmotivating, all those solemn and dire warnings. Sounds more like a doomsday event than a flu epidemic."

"Well, I think this coronavirus has given society a solid reality check. Our lives, our health, our economy are all subject to change, and life is about accepting that we aren't in control and embracing rather than rejecting change."

Ron nodded in agreement, so much so that Garret laughed and pointed it out. "Ron, if you keep nodding so much, you're going to become a bobblehead."

Standing straight up, Ron saluted his boss and sat back down, returning to his work, wincing as he got uncomfortably stuck in his small chair again. Squirming around, he ended with a slightly slouching position, quietly grumbling about his back pain.

The assignment for Ron was to identify the lowest-cost commodity chain link to supply materials for the company's above-ground wiring. For the plastic outer tubing of the wires, he found a company in Burnaby that outsourced the material from a factory in China. There were several other manufacturers in the Richmond industrial area, but they were nearly 25 percent more expensive than their Chinese counterparts. Of course, the shipping of the material from China would have to be included in the cost-benefit comparison, but by buying in bulk, the economies of scale savings would be good for BC Electric.

Copying down the Burnaby company's contact number and email, Ron printed it off and filed it in his folder to be returned to Garret for approval.

As for the copper wiring, Ron identified several dirt-cheap scrapyards offering the raw material, but he knew that those recycling yards tended to be havens for criminals to sell their stolen copper and steel.

Finding a more ethical source in the United States, he opted for one close to the border to minimize transport costs and ensure a more reliable, quicker source of raw material. Adding the American supplier to the list on his chain, Ron finished the analysis by filing its contact information along with the rest of the companies.

Waiting for Garret to finish a conversation, Ron stared at the clock on the wall.

"Ron, even if you keep looking at that clock, it won't go a second faster," Garret said.

Ron nodded in embarrassment at having been caught twice already and handed Garret the file containing his analysis of the supply chain, saying, "Here's the analysis optimizing the best supply chains in consideration of cost and ethically sourced materials. The conclusion and the results of the analysis should be on the last page. In short, outsourcing outside Canada might be our only option, as most companies here subcontract out the job outside Canada anyways."

"Thanks. Go on home," Garret said. "You're off, man!"

"Appreciate it, Garret! See you tomorrow!"

Donning a windbreaker jacket, one size too small, just as he liked it, Ron headed out into the rain, went to his car, and drove to the gym. There were still two hours left before badminton training started, so Ron decided to train for a bit at his regular fitness gym.

After hanging up his jacket, he warmed up on the treadmill. He noticed that one of the girls in the gym was looking at him. Feeling a bit embarrassed, he focused on the exercise, blushing slightly from the attention.

After nearly two months of rehab and nearly three years of retraining, Ron was more muscular than he'd been before he got sick, and he was attracting a fair amount of attention from the women.

On two occasions now, girls who were working out had asked for his number, but he politely declined, saying he already had someone in his heart. It wasn't because he didn't feel attracted to the women. Rather, he felt like he was abandoning Penny and cruelly forgetting her. He wanted to remember her forever, to never let her go.

Following the treadmill, Ron opted for some arm exercises, using the bench press. He put roughly one-hundred-and-eighty-five pounds on the bar and, lying down on the rest, gripped the bar with the weights and pressed twenty-five repetitions. After each set of reps, he took a break, then started another set of twenty-five. Soon enough his arms were sore, and he decided to work on his lower body with the leg press. This time, setting around two-hundred-and-fifty pounds, he did five sets of twenty reps, the weights making a pang sound each time he released the load. Lastly, he worked on his core, sitting on a mat and doing twenty sets of sit-ups, with each set consisting of twenty-five repetitions.

After changing into a fresh set of clothes, Ron headed for his second workout—badminton training. This time, the repetitions weren't in twenty-fives or fifteens, but in the hundreds. One hundred smashes, one hundred clears, one hundred drops—nearly one hundred in each technique or skill. Ron stopped counting after a thousand hits and just resigned himself to hitting any birdie back no matter what number it was.

In addition to the satisfaction of training, Ron was glad to see Xu had come back to training badminton after staying in the hospital for several weeks. Xu still wasn't as fit as he'd been before, but Coach Lucas was willing to keep him on as a confidence booster for the team, who were all concerned for Xu. He'd come a long way, from being on life support with a ventilator to now running around playing badminton.

The good news was that only Xu had gotten sick out of the whole team, and he'd been tested early enough to avoid transmitting the disease to any other players. The Sports Competition was only seven months away, having been delayed for a year due to COVID-19.

Everyone on the team was excited; for some, it was the first time they would be out of the country. Ron, though, had been to Hong Kong, Ketchikan, Los Angeles, and some other cities. Nonetheless, he was still excited to go to Tokyo. This excitement translated to extra hard work by everyone, so as not to disappoint Canada, which they were representing.

"Alright, everyone, skill training finished," the coach called out. "Let's move on to practice games, alright? Lucy and Ron, play singles on court one, team Steve against team Xu on court two, and lastly, the women's double team will face off against me on court three."

On court one, Ron was eager for an official training

match, as drills and training could be repetitive and quite boring. Lucy served first. Starting the match, she hit a high serve to Ron's backcourt. He got back in time and replied with a punch clear, shooting the birdie to the far backline. Lucy then did a sharp drop, hoping to catch Ron deep in the court. But with his fast footwork, he was ready and returned the drop with another drop, forcing Lucy to come forward. Having done the damage with the first drop shot, Lucy's return was too weak, and Ron smashed the shuttle down in a thunderous shot that landed in. Several other smashes also thundered down, and soon the score was at game point—twenty for Ron and fifteen for Lucy. Saving his trademark serve for last, Ron hit an underhand serve from near his waist, standing farther behind to give a better angle and making the shuttle fly flat near the tip of the net—which was near impossible to return. Indeed, Lucy missed the shot, which ended the match.

The next game resulted in a similar score, and both Ron and Lucy felt they were mutually improving, getting better and better thanks to the practice.

"Alright, everyone," Coach Lucas said. "Let's call it a night! Good job, guys. See you all tomorrow at six sharp!"

Ron changed for the third time, this time into a polo shirt and jeans, which was by far the most comfortable in the spring weather. After saying goodbye to Lucy, Xu, Steve, and the rest of the team, he headed for home, tired and eager to have a nice, hot dinner courtesy of Mom.

Arriving back home, he dropped off his gym bag in the hallway and sprinted up the stairs to shower.

"Ron! Dinner is in fifteen minutes, okay?" his mom called after him.

"Yes, Ma, I'm just going to shower first."

Walking over to Ron's gym bag, Dad made a disgusted face after smelling a waft of it. "Phew, it smells like old socks!" Taking an air freshener, he viciously attacked the bag with sprays of Hawaiian breeze scent till the whole hallway reeked of peaches and mango.

Mom walked right into the air trap, choking and holding her nose. "Honey! What did you do? Blah, it smells like rotten fruit! I can't breathe! Gah!" Opening a window near the kitchen, she sucked in mouthfuls of air, not knowing what was worse—Ron's bag or the suffocating air freshener.

A few minutes later, Ron bounded down the stairs, struggling to pull his undersized shirt over his muscular body. "Blah! What's that smell, Dad?" Ron's shirt was half on and half off, so Dad helped him by pulling the back down, freeing his son from the confines of his shirt.

"Phew, it smells like mangos," Ron said. "Thanks, Dad. Maybe it's time to get some new clothes. I barely fit in most of them now."

"That's a blessing in disguise. Most of your clothes were bought a year ago, when you were a bit less toned," His dad said with a chuckle.

"Guess what? Another girl at the gym asked for my number ..." Ron trailed off as his parents looked at him worriedly, in case he'd reminded himself of Penny.

"Well, did you give it?" Dad asked.

"Give what?"

"Your number? To the girl?"

"Well, I kinda said I already had someone in my heart."

Dad and Mom exchanged glances again and got back to what they had been preoccupied with, trying desperately to avoid the inevitable outcome.

"Mom, Dad, don't worry. I'm fine. I've learned to move on." Ron smiled hesitantly at his parents.

"Well, to celebrate moving on, let's start dinner! Today, we have beef and broccoli with garlic, spaghetti Bolognese, and steamed halibut with soy sauce and sautéed green onions," Mom announced.

Both son and father clapped their hands at her presentation, and as she put out the last of the dishes, both couldn't wait to dive into the delicious meal.

While potatoes were Dad's favourite vegetable, his favourite meat by far was fish: salmon, trout, halibut, and snapper were common dishes he really enjoyed. Ron started with the beef and broccoli, covered with a gravy-like sauce and minced garlic. He relished the dish's salty and sweet flavour combination.

When he was ready, Dad dove right for the fish, first taking the cheeks, called *meen gun,* before taking a large section of the tail end. The fish was flaky and moist, and the sweet soy sauce complemented the roasted garlic and sautéed green onions. Ron went for the Bolognese next, showing his inner Italian. The meat sauce was loose and not chunky, the cheese was melted and crusted on the top, and it all had the correct ratio of tomatoes to meat. Using a fork, Ron spun a ball of spaghetti onto his plate and started slurping up the pasta, getting tomato sauce on his nose. Wiping it off, he smiled sheepishly at his parents before tucking back in to his pasta.

The meat on the fish disappeared rapidly as Dad devoured the meal with gusto. Pretty soon he was flipping over the fish to start on the backside of it, but this time, he gave Mom the cheek, politely putting it on her plate while smiling. But after dropping off the fish, he sneakily took a piece of beef Mom had on her plate and relished the stolen morsel.

"It seems we have a robber in our midst," Mom said to Ron, looking for his opinion. But Ron simply kept eating, not making eye contact and avoiding the ever-more embarrassing situation.

"Oh, please forgive this robber. I come bringing a humble offering," Dad said, taking a piece of beef and feeding it to Mom. She fluttered her eyelids at him, accepting the gift.

Ron kept his head down, pretending not to have noticed the flirting.

After his second bowl of rice, Ron was pretty full. In fact, it was a rare occasion when he ate more than two bowls. He had started off eating one and a half bowls two years before, but with his new regimen and training, he was able to stomach two bowls both for lunch and dinner, burning off most of the carbs.

Ron enjoyed eating rice, having grown up eating jasmine rice. The slight fragrance and shorter kernels made it his favourite type.

As was tradition, he ended the meal with *fan suew* that had soaked in the rice pot for some time. He breathed in the delicious aroma of browned, roasted rice that rose from their bowls in wafts of steam. Slurping the water, he tried to be as quiet as possible, slightly embarrassed because of how loud he was. He remembered how Penny disapproved of his loud slurping—whether it was soup, water, or broth. She always laughed at him, telling him to drink quietly, but the more she laughed, the louder he purposely slurped, just to annoy her in a flirting way. She, of course, often got him back, one time tipping the soup bowl he was slurping from and causing half of it to land on his shirt. As he quietly sipped his rice water, Ron smiled as he remembered those happy moments.

Finishing the day after a delicious dinner, everyone went about their chores and prepared for the next day. Pretty soon, they all retired for the night, looking forward to another day, eager to face its challenges and accept its surprises.

With Saturday off from work, Ron was outside with Mom in the garden, where she grew vegetables, herbs, and a variety of fruits. He decided to spend the time off with her, following her as she went about her daily and weekly tasks.

Mom harvested some of the last snow peas, some of which were beginning to turn yellow from old age and were starting to get tough.

The snow peas started from a single seed, then grew creepers that became anchors for the plant itself, allowing it to grow taller and taller. The plant produced small white flowers that, when pollinated, died off and transformed into small pods that eventually become the edible snow peas. Not only were the pods edible, but the tender shoots of the plant, *doaw mew,* were also highly prized in Chinese cuisine, selling for a premium at Asian grocery stores.

Using a pair of pruning scissors, Mom gathered some green onions, cutting them near the stem. The robust plants grew back very quickly after being harvested, and it was possible to harvest them three or four times in a single season, given favourable growing conditions.

Ron went over to a garlic plant and pulled one out with ease, but he was dismayed to see the garlic cloves were far too tiny to be harvested.

"It's far too early for the garlic, Son," Mom said. "We just planted them several weeks ago. They'll need at least a few more weeks before we can eat them. Here, give me that plant."

Ron handed it over to Mom, and she delicately planted it back into the soil and patted the edges to make sure there weren't any air pockets.

"If you want to put your strength to good use," she said, "why don't you pull those potatoes up? Careful not to detach the spuds from the plant itself; otherwise, we'll be playing treasure hunting in the soil."

Ron slowly unearthed a potato plant, and suddenly a whole network of potatoes appeared from the soil, clinging to the main stem. Smiling at his accomplishment, he put his harvest into the basket.

"Ron, just take the potatoes. Pull apart the plant and roots and throw them into the composter. No honey, that's the garbage, dear. The composter is the black-looking cylinder thing. Just open the hatch. There you go."

Having gotten his hands dirty, he continued working by pulling potato plants; it was fun to be so productive and actually harvesting food they would be eating. Taking a break, he marveled at the wooden trellis that helped the beans and snow peas crawl up.

Mom, seeing him notice the trellis, remarked, "Your dad made that. Nearly banged up his thumb, but it's very sturdy." As she leaned on it to try to prove the point, there was a slight cracking sound. She backed off immediately, looking very much embarrassed.

Laughing with his mother, Ron noticed the small cherry tomatoes dangling in sets of twelve or so. "Should I pick some tomatoes, Mom?" Before she answered, he plucked one, shined it on his shirt, and promptly ate it with relish.

"Just take one or two sets," she said. "We keep them on the vine so they taste better after ripening. Don't take too much. Otherwise we'll just end up wasting them."

Popping another into his mouth, Ron smiled with tomato seeds between his teeth.

Mom looked up and just laughed, continuing to unearth some carrots.

Ron placed his two vines of tomatoes into the basket and saw the carrots Mom had pulled up, which looked very irregular and strange.

"Mom, why do those carrots have legs? They look like stickmen …"

"Honestly, I'm not sure. Sometimes they look normal,

other times they grow multiple limbs. It just might be the type of seeds we used, but I'm not certain."

"I thought you were the master gardener, Mom. Don't you know everything about growing?"

"That would be your great-aunts. They owned large vegetable farms in Surrey; they're the professional growers, not me. My skills are more in the arts and crafts sector, but thanks for the vote of confidence. Remember the gift I made for you last year? Those wool socks?"

Ron's expression changed to mock horror as he recalled the ugly socks. "Mom! Why did you make me remember those horrid socks? My mind will be forever scarred with the image of them—truly the ugliest socks I'd ever seen!"

Mom pretended to frown, keeping her laughter muffled. "Is that how you thank me for slaving away to make those socks for you?" Unable to contain her laughter, she burst out laughing as Ron threw an unripe tomato at her.

Seeing a snail crawl towards the snow peas, Ron plucked it by its shell and launched it into the forest next to the garden.

Ron knew Dad had always been fascinated by little critters, such as ants, spiders, pill bugs and grasshoppers. Ever since Ron was a little kid, Dad had always shown him the plethora of insects in their garden, catching them with his bare hands.

They once found a dragonfly that had a damaged wing. Dad carefully took it to his insectarium and placed water and food for the carnivore. To Dad's disappointment, the dragonfly didn't survive, being too wild to be domesticated and unable to recover from its injured wing. Dad's fascination with wildlife included animals, too, and Ron remembered the painted-face turtle they had for several years, which lived in the backyard pond. Dad fed the turtle strawberries that would float for a while before being ambushed from below by the turtle. When it eventually died, Dad buried it in the garden, forever remembering it by the name he had given it: James the turtle. It was the only turtle Dad ever had.

Ron looked over to where Dad had buried James, but then a ladybug caught his attention, landing on the rose plant next to Ron. The rosebuds were just starting to be infested with aphids as late summer crept closer and closer. The parasites would soon multiply profusely in the hot summer weather.

Ants were busy farming the aphids for the dew they secreted, and in return, the ants protected the aphids from predators—like the ladybug.

The red beetle began devouring the plump, slow-moving aphids, which were too slow to even run away. After the sixth or seventh aphid was eaten, the ants noticed the threat to their animal farm and started to chase away the ladybug. It had a hard shell, and the ants' bites did not deter it one bit. But its legs were vulnerable to being pulled off by ants. When it was starting to get swarmed by the aggressive insects, the ladybug opened its wings and flew away, having stolen a full meal from the ants.

Dad not only studied ants when he was young, he also collected them in ant farms, which were containers designed to show the labyrinth ants build underneath the surface of the ground. The ants were captured then transported to the container, and Dad would watch them dig various tunnels to form their underground chambers. But these colonies would never last, as there was no queen to replenish them.

Mom told Ron once that Grandma threw away Dad's ant farm when he did something particularly bad. Dad was extremely upset, crying out of anger and sorrow because of Grandma's discipline.

Ron recalled seeing the only picture of his grandparents from his father's side hanging on the wall in the hallway. His grandfather was a tall, jolly man with a tremendous smile, while Grandma had a stern, disciplinary look on her face. Dad's arm was on Grandpa's shoulders, and he had an awkward smile, as Dad always had the worst of any natural smiles. His eyes and posture showed a distancing from Grandma—an untold chasm that existed between them. Behind his eyes, Dad hid a multitude of painful memories that Ron found out about only from Mom. Dad couldn't even bear to tell him face-to-face.

Propelling another snail into the shrubbery, Ron tested the weight of the basket and was pleasantly surprised at how heavy it was. "This would make a great dumbbell, just lifting this basket with one arm."

Mom didn't even need to say anything; her frown and the shaking of her head told him he would be in big, big trouble if he even tried such a stunt.

Slightly disappointed at being refused permission, Ron opted to lift a boulder as a test of his strength. Flexing his arms, he took hold of the rock and lifted it, setting it to one side, astonished at the creatures that were underneath it.

"Mom, look! A huge slug … It's ugly. Looks like a piece of manure with marbling."

Walking over to Ron, Mom nodded in acknowledgement. "That's a banana slug. It's known to grow larger than regular slugs. Yes, they're quite disgusting, not to mention devastating to our crops. Here, take a hand shovel and fling it into the forest, alright?"

Ron's eyes lit up with anticipation. Setting the slug into his shovel, he braced his arm and launched the slug high into the sky towards the grove of trees.

"Good riddance," Mom said. "And oh, Ron, look here. There's an albino pill bug! It's really rare to see one, you know." The bug Mom was pointing to was slightly orange in colour, different from the other pill bugs, which were bluish-grey. It bumbled and jostled among the other pill bugs, slugs, earthworms, and millipedes—all disturbed by the sudden exposure to the light. They scampered here and there, seeking a new place of refuge from the scorching afternoon sun, as they usually came out only after dusk to feed.

"You know, your dad used to go out in his parents' garden in the wee morning hours to hunt for slugs eating his snow peas and vegetables. He wasn't a good gardener, but he gets really excited about watching crops grow and spending time to take care of them."

Ron was astonished. "Dad, a gardener? Unbelievable!"

From their experience, any plants that were put under Dad's care tended to wither, rot, and die, with the household cactus the only exception.

Laughing, Mom went over to the blueberry bush to see if any new berries were ripe enough to pick.

"Here, Ron, try a blueberry. This one should be ripe enough to be sweet. You can usually tell by how dark blue the berry is."

She handed him the berry, and he promptly tossed it in the air and caught it in his mouth.

"Mmmm it's sweet! Wasn't that the blueberry bush we pruned last year?" he said.

"Yes, it is. That's why there are so many berries this season. Pruning them encourages new growth and more flowers—meaning more berries as well."

Flicking another snail into the bushes, Ron saw a spider and watched as it trapped some winged insect and wrapped it around and around in sticky silk. "Didn't you once tell me Dad was fascinated with spiders as well when he was young?" he asked.

"He used to feed the spiders, watching them trap and eat bugs that he tossed into their webs. He was especially fascinated with wolf spiders, trying to lure them out of their holes with bugs in their cone-like webs."

"Speaking of spiders, I'm playing this new game right now. In it, you get to battle giant spiders, ants, aphids, and other insects."

"You can always play the more serene farming games, you know, like the ones I play."

"Yeah, I prefer the more peaceful games, rather than those psychological horror games," Ron replied.

"Your dad was pretty traumatized as a kid after watching some horror movies. He had nightmares of a dinosaur eye appearing in his parents' bedroom window, or getting sucked into a magical board game in the basement."

"Really? Wow. Perhaps I should dress up as a dinosaur on Dad's birthday? Is he still afraid of them even now?"

"Monsters don't scare him anymore. He's not the same scared little kid that I heard his mother tell me about. He's much more courageous and even protective of us, his family. He's a good father, you know, because ... Well, he's been through a lot, which helped teach him more about life." Smiling proudly at thoughts of her husband, Mom continued to gladly praise his good qualities, telling Ron he should learn from his father.

"You know, I think we have enough vegetables for the week. What do you think?" she finally said.

Ron grabbed a handful of blueberries and started gobbling them up, talking between mouthfuls. "Mmmm, yeah I think we have enough."

"Dear, you'd better wash your teeth after. You've got blueberry everywhere in your mouth," she told him. Laughing after seeing Ron smile with his blueberry stains, she gathered the gloves and shovels and indicated to him to grab the basket of vegetables.

As he grabbed the harvested crop, an ant crawled up the

basket handle onto Ron's hand. "Shoo, you little bugger, be gone with you!" Blowing at the ant, he managed to get rid of it and continued bringing the basket back to the house.

"I thought you liked ants. Why so scared?" Ron asked.

"It's a love-hate relationship, honestly. I like watching them work. Just not crawling over my body. Even thinking of it gives me the shivers."

Ron smiled as he followed Mom back inside, but his smile disappeared when he saw Dad watching the TV. He had a face of seriousness and indignation. It was evident something was terribly wrong.

"Dad, what's wrong? Isn't that—?" Ron's voice froze as he saw the TV and listened to the broadcaster telling the breaking-news story.

"Thirty-year-old Kun-sun Roe, convicted of one count of dangerous operation of a vehicle, was just given parole after serving nearly two and a half years of prison time," the reporter said. "She was convicted after crashing with a red sedan near Kensington Polytechnic University, causing the driver, Penny Ma, to sustain life-threatening injuries, which she later succumbed to in hospital."

Ron slowly put down the basket and sat down, paralyzed by the injustice he'd just witnessed and unable to speak while he was in shock at the news.

CHAPTER 14

ENEMIES

As the early summer days got warmer, to Ron, something cold happened as he watched Kun-sun hurry out of the courthouse on the TV news.

"Miss Roe, do you wish to make a statement? How do you feel about causing this tragedy? What do you want to say to Miss Ma's family?"

A flurry of reporters surrounded Kun-sun as she speed-walked to her waiting car. Her lawyer protected her somewhat from the crowd, but cameras and microphones were everywhere, following the convicted killer.

She was stone-faced, without an ounce of emotion. She tried not to look at the mob behind her, which did nothing to deter the constant flashing of cameras.

With Kun-sun whisked away, the reporters turned to the victim's family, asking for any comment on the parole hearing.

"We're terribly saddened by the outcome, and we just wish the justice system would do its job and enforce justice—justice for Penny—and not let dangerous drivers back on the road," one of Penny's relatives said.

Kun-sun Roe.

Just the thought of her name made Ron uneasy. He was angry, frustrated, disappointed, and ultimately hurt over why someone could be so reckless as to drive while drunk, ultimately taking a life because of their irresponsibility. While he realized that his hospitalization was partly to blame, he saw the tragedy as mostly Kun-sun's fault, due to her dangerous driving. If he ever saw her, he would give her a piece of his mind, telling her how much she had taken away from him. He wanted her to know that he would never be the same. Two and a half years was simply not enough to compensate for Penny's death. Nothing could bring her back. Nothing could fill that void in Ron's life.

A day later, still mesmerized by the shock of the news about Penny's killer, Ron was glued to the TV set, hoping for some correction or appeal to overturn the court decision.

Mom put her hand on his shoulder, patting him. "Come, have something to eat, Ron. It's been nearly a day since you last ate. You need strength to push on. Penny would want you to stay strong."

As he slowly got up from the chair, Ron's tearstained face quivered as he headed towards the dining table. Picking up a bowl of rice, he started eating slowly, in complete silence.

Mom looked in semi-relief towards Dad, glad that their son was finally eating again, but worried about his depressed state of mind.

Lying on his bed, Ron prepared himself so that he could go back to work the next day. He would have to put aside his feelings and act in a professional and dignified manner. Washing the tear stains off his face, he decided to move on with a fresh start in the morning, knowing that his sadness couldn't fully be washed away with any amount of water. Waiting for sleep to take him away from his sadness, Ron fell asleep, starting a recurring yet confusing dream.

Ron saw Penny and her two kids again, and they were following the short man again. This time they walked to a cliff, when suddenly there was a quake, and Penny and her kids were left dangling on the edge.

The man at first appeared to help, but then he shied away and cowardly ran off, leaving them behind.

Then, Kun-sun came, with an evil smile on her face. She took out a pocketknife and began sawing away at the rope Penny and her kids were holding on to.

Ron screamed in anger and frustration, trying to get to them, stop Kun-sun, and save Penny and the children. But by the time he got to the edge, Kun-sun had cut the rope and Ron could helplessly do nothing, watching Penny and her kids fall into the dark canyon below.

Crying in his sleep, his tears rolled down his face and disappeared into his pillow, one by one, as he tried to ease his pain by sleeping.

At work, he was also dozing, until a familiar voice woke him up.

"Ron, Ron?"

Ron looked up from his desk and grimaced at having been caught nodding off. He was no longer in his bed at home, but was dozing in the office, much to his embarrassment.

"It looks like someone could use some coffee, eh?" Rhonda smiled at him, gently pushing him.

"Hey, hey, remember to physically distance," Ron said. "I do need coffee. I didn't sleep well last night. So where did you guys go for your honeymoon? A staycation due to COVID-19?"

Rhonda rolled her eyes with annoyance. "Don't even get me started! We had to cancel our trip to sunny Cancun, Mexico, and settle for smoky interior BC and its forest fires. We had to stay indoors for most of the time, and when we were allowed out it was suffocating." Shaking her head, she walked away, grumbling to herself.

Smiling, Ron walked over to the break room, took a coffee pod, and started making a large cup of breakfast-style coffee. Looking over at the jar of pickled kidney beans, he gagged slightly, trying not to throw up his breakfast, as the beans had been there for over a week.

Averting his gaze and taking four lumps of sugar and two creams, he waited for the machine to finish sputtering out his drink. With his cup in hand, he walked to his desk and checked what he was working on before he had dozed off. Grateful for the new chair that was big enough to accommodate his large frame, he comfortably sat by the computer, checking the latest numbers and responding to emails.

Hearing some commotion, Ron looked over to where two associates were discussing the latest joke of the day posted on the wall.

"What insect helps protect your roofs from getting clogged and flooding? Leaf gutter ants," one said, laughing.

His coworker chuckled. "Wow, it's so stupid it's hilarious! Hey, here's another one: What plant protects your roof night and day? The tree guard gutter system!"

Unable to contain their laughter, the workers belted out hoots and hollers, laughing at the jokes. Both bent over double in fits of laughter. The supervising manager, Garret, walked over to see what the commotion was about. One associate was still trying to quell his laughter, while his coworker patted him on the back, trying to help. Pretty soon, even Garret was laughing politely, joining in with the joke-making.

"You know why the dandelion left the lawn? Because it was too arrogant and grass!" Garret said.

Everyone was looking slightly puzzled at the joke, not

quite understanding it. Meanwhile, Garret alone laughed at his own joke. "Get it? Crass, grass? Oh c'mon, guys."

Ron shook his head, smiling at the embarrassed manager. Walking over, he tried to save the disgraced joke maker with one of his own. "Guys, guys, let's leaf him be."

Rhonda took a second before understanding Ron's joke. She laughed and said, "That's a good one, bud."

Soon everyone was dispersing from the hallway and heading back to work.

Going to the bathroom, Ron felt the effects of his coffee. The caffeine ensured several more trips to the washroom before everything was stable. For the fourth time, he went into the middle stall and noticed some scratched writing on the wall: "Garret is a stupid idiot!"

Wondering who might have written those comments, Ron went over to Garret's office to let him know about the mutinous words. Seeing his boss was in a conversation, Ron waited outside for a bit before entering and unintentionally overheard Garret speaking.

"Walter, you know we don't accept foul language, horseplay, or crude behaviour here. If I catch you emailing anyone with crude remarks or jokes, or even disrespecting a fellow employee, I'll have to let you go. This is your final warning, Walter."

Bang!

Walter stormed out of the office in a rage, making every head rise above the cubicles like gophers to see what had happened. Ron cautiously walked into the office, seeing Garret shaking his head and looking down.

"Garret, I'm sorry if this is a bad time, but, I just noticed some profanity in the washroom directed against, um, you."

The supervising manager smiled and looked up at Ron. "Yes, I noticed that myself. Thanks for letting me know, Ron." Looking back down, he returned to his paperwork while

Ron left the office feeling helpless to stem the war between Walter and the company management.

Silently grateful he wasn't working next to Walter, Ron could still hear the man complaining to his coworkers loudly. "Such a stupid, senseless manager. Always so blunderingly serious. Can't even take a joke. If I were manager, we'd be having fun, making everyone laugh. Not being silenced like idiots in a curfew."

Trying to tune out the whining, Ron focused on his work, hoping to finish the analysis by the end of the workday. This time the analysis was focusing on the costs and benefits of outsourcing tech support services to India. The cost of an online customer service technician was nearly 40 percent cheaper in the newly developing country than in Canada. The problem was that the image of the company would be negatively impacted if news of outsourcing was leaked out to the public; people wanted jobs to stay in Canada and, more particularly, in BC. Ron figured that customers would be willing to pay a premium for local service agents and that the cost savings of outsourcing wouldn't be beneficial, all things considered. But even within Canada, the costs of hiring service agents were not the same; the average salary in the prairies and Atlantic Canada were slightly less than their counterparts on the West Coast, Ontario, and Quebec.

Finishing his report, Ron concluded that outsourcing the jobs to other parts of Canada might be acceptable, but outsourcing outside Canada wouldn't be beneficial, especially for the company's reputation among local customers.

Printing the report for Garret to review, Ron walked to the printers and noticed there was a line waiting for the printer.

"Looks like there's a black Friday sale going on, eh?" said a staffer waiting in line.

A coworker rolled his eyes and lamented, "Some smart

aleck decided to print a couple hundred pages. It's ridiculous. I've been waiting for nearly fifteen minutes now, and the line hasn't budged a bit!"

"Where's the person printing the large load? Maybe he'll let us print our documents first since we only need a couple of pages," Ron said—a suggestion that was agreed upon as a good idea.

Another coworker farther up the line looked back and agreed. "Yeah, that would be a good idea, but I have no clue who printed the pages."

As Ron walked to the front of the line, he saw that everyone seemed to be waiting, and the owner of the large print load didn't seem to be in line. Taking one of the pages just printed, he noticed they were from an instructor manual for employee training.

"What in the world?" he muttered. "Who's printing out employee manuals? And more than one of them!" Looking through the printed pages, he counted nearly ten manuals printed. Pressing the cancel button, he looked at the printer and tried to identify which computer initiated the request.

The display screen said, "Printing initiated by Terminal 6."

"Alright, whose computer is terminal six?" he asked. "Who printed out all these manuals?"

A few employees were silently pointing to the corner cubicle—Walter Campbell's cubicle.

Walking over to Walter, Ron confronted him directly. "Why on earth are you printing out so many employee manuals, Walter? Do you want me to tell Garret?"

Walter silently typed away at his computer, ignoring Ron's accusations. Head held high and bent on getting revenge on Garret, Walter had a sense of arrogance about him that made Ron feel uneasy.

"You leave me no choice, buddy," Ron said. "I'll give you

one last chance. You can tell Garret yourself, or I'll do it for you."

Walter turned around, as cold and emotionless as a stone, his eyes empty. Then he turned back to his computer without a care in the world.

Ron shook his head and went to tell Garret, figuring this would be the last straw before he would fire Walter.

Many heads were nodding, approving of Ron's handling of the situation and relieved that the office troublemaker would finally be condemned.

"I see, thank you for bringing this to my attention, Ron," Garret said after hearing the story. "What do you think I should do? Should I let him go or give him another lecture—and another chance?"

"Honestly, Garret, you've given him many, many chances, and he has no intention of changing his wrongdoings. If you don't let him go, I think it would send a bad message to the other employees."

"Alright, I'll make my decision shortly. You can go back to work."

Walking out of the office, Ron could feel a pair of eyes staring at the back of his head. Turning around, he could see Walter's threatening glare, no longer emotionless, but now full of rage and anger. Avoiding making eye contact with the man, Ron glanced at Rhonda, who nervously smiled, mouthing the words "Be careful" before turning back to her computer.

When Ron went back to the printer, he found the line had dispersed, so he collected his report from the tray. Glancing through the pages, he noticed that the sixth page was missing. Looking throughout the tray, he realized it was nowhere to be seen, Someone had taken it.

Confused as to what happened, he had to print out page six again. This time he was able to collect it and insert it into his report. Knocking on Garret's door, he got the all clear to come in, and he handed the report to his manager.

"Thanks, Ron. Oh, and I'd avoid talking to Walter even after he's let go. He's got it in for you. So just be careful, okay?"

Ron flexed his arms and showed them off to Garret. "He'll have to get past my guns to hurt me."

Garret smiled and laughed at Ron's confidence in his strength. While watching Ron leave, Garret wished the situation wouldn't come to requiring self-defence. He just hoped firing Walter was the right thing to do.

Ron went to clear his desk, throwing out the coffee cup and giving the surface a disinfectant wipe-down. Reusable coffee mugs were no longer permitted due to COVID-19, and disinfecting shared areas was mandatory now. Watching the clock, Ron had about five minutes before he could clock out, so he decided to watch the TV in the break room. When he walked in and looked up at the screen, he was astonished by what he saw: the man in his dreams, the one stealing his family, was being arrested for sexual assault.

CHAPTER 15

REVELATIONS

"Joe Chandler, a thirty-one-year-old old man from Surrey, was arrested today for sexually assaulting a girl at a shopping mall," the reporter said. "Police say he is known to them and has been convicted of at least three other sex assaults spanning a period of seven years from 2013 to 2019."

The bag Ron was holding dropped silently, his thoughts frozen as he stared like a statue at the man being handcuffed. His mouth opened, but no sound came out. He was so shocked that he simply stood there for several minutes before clocking out and speeding back home, ignoring badminton practice. On the car's Bluetooth, he called Dad and let him know what he'd seen.

"Yes, Dad, I'm sure it was him. I saw him in my dreams multiple times. Yes, it's on the news. Can't you see it? I'm almost home."

Pulling into the driveway, Ron rushed inside, went upstairs, grabbed his laptop, and rushed down to show his parents. Going to the local news website, he clicked on the article and pointed at the man being arrested in the photo.

"That's him. He was the one in my dreams taking away Penny and her kids. And I noticed that one of the kids had blond hair like his, not black like mine or Penny's."

Hot tears of anger began rolling down Ron's face. Mom walked over and offered a hug, having understood the implications of what they'd just realized.

"I have to call Penny's parents," Ron said. "They might know something about it. Maybe they could shed some light on what went on."

Dad took hold of Ron's arm and looked him right in the eye. "Son, are you sure you want to know the truth? I mean, can you handle it, however bad it may be?"

"I think I've been having all those dreams for a reason, and now's my chance to figure out what really went on and get some closure. I need this, Dad. Please."

Dad let go of his son and nodded, agreeing with him. So Ron dialled Mr. and Mrs. Ma's number.

"Hello, Ron," Penny's mom said when she answered.

"Hi, Mrs. Ma. How are you and Mr. Ma doing?" Ron took a second to wipe the tears from his face.

"We're getting by, day by day. I hope you're managing well?"

"I'm doing alright. But there's a question I wanted to ask. You see, I just saw on the news about a man who sexually assaulted several women over six years. Also, I've been having these dreams, seeing Penny and two kids walking with that rapist. Was Penny … Was she sexually assaulted?"

The other side of the line became quiet, and Ron could hear a distant discussion between Mrs. and Mr. Ma.

"Ron, we just wanted to say thank you for being there for our Penny while you two were together," Mrs. Ma said. "We hoped you both would start a wonderful, loving family, and we never expected the worst would happen. But in regards to your question, yes, she was raped in early 2017 before you entered the hospital. I'm sorry, Ron. We didn't tell you. We didn't want to worry you further."

This time it was Ron's side of the line that was silent. He sobbed as he digested the horrific news. "Was … Was Penny pregnant?"

Another long, awkward pause staunched the conversation. But the tone was serious and truthful, and both sides were starting to feel closure.

"Yes, Ron, she had just tested positive for being pregnant roughly a month before the crash."

Ron was shocked. He had talked with Penny a month before the crash, and she didn't tell him about any of this. She must have been hiding so much pain and hurt. How in the world was she able to still smile and encourage him after what happened to her?

"Thank you, Mr. Ma. I … I appreciate you telling me what happened."

"We're sorry we didn't tell you earlier, but it wasn't your fault, Ron. There was nothing you could have done to prevent what happened."

"Thank you." Ron began sobbing again.

"Take care, Ron."

As he hung up the phone, Mom and Dad hugged him again, having heard every gut-wrenching word that was said.

"I don't understand … She never told me … She was there for me, but I wasn't there for her when she needed me most." Ron sobbed into his dad's shoulder, his shirt muffling his cries.

Mom patted Ron on the back, rubbing his shoulders. "Ron, remember, it wasn't your fault and there's nothing you could have done. I'm sorry you had to go through all this … All this pain and suffering, but you've been through the worst of it. You can get through this part as well … There, there." Hugging her son, she let his tears fall onto her shoulder, mourning with him and caring for him during his grieving process.

"I think I'm going to lie down for a while. Thanks, Mom." He walked up the stairs ever so slowly, then closed his room door and lay on his bed.

Taking out his phone, he looked back to one of the last pictures of him and Penny, roughly two weeks before her crash. Ron had the goofiest smile, and Penny looked so content, so joyous, so happy despite having the memories of what had happened to her a couple of weeks prior. She was not only happy but she made him happy as well, sharing the infectious emotion with those around her.

Joe Chandler, Ron thought.

He stole from Penny what should have been for her husband. Worst of all, Ron would no longer be able to be with Penny. They couldn't get married, they couldn't have a family. And what hope and aspirations had been left were dashed by Penny's crash.

Ring, ring!

Picking up his smartphone, Ron saw it was Coach Lucas, and he quickly answered it.

"Hi, Coach, sorry I couldn't make it to practice today. I had some bad news come up about Penny. I'll try to come tomorrow though."

"Don't worry, Ron. We know if you're not here it must be something important. But don't worry yourself about practice, settle what you have to do first and we can talk about training again later. Cheers."

"Thanks, Coach." Ron lay back on the bed, thinking of what might have been and what was going to be. Letting his memories of Penny fade, he nodded off, having attained closure to his visions and dreams, understanding now why they'd haunted him for so long. Drifting off to sleep, he subtly smiled, with a single tear falling, free from the nightmares of his past and able to finally move on.

Waking up the next morning with a yawn, Ron felt refreshed—ready to start the day and take on whatever challenges might come. There was no more nightmare, no images of Joe, just good old-fashioned restful sleep, with dreams of playing badminton in the Sports Competition and attending summer camps as a kid.

Bounding down the stairs once again, he felt lighter, as if some unseen burden had been finally lifted from his back.

Mom shook her head in disapproval but smiled, glad to see her son was happy and in good spirits. Dad, too, was glad, especially because Ron's mourning process was over and he finally comprehended what his dreams were about and had attained closure.

Ron planted a kiss on Mom's cheek, took a plate of breakfast, and sat next to Dad. Taking the ketchup bottle, he squeezed a smiley face on the omelet, complete with eyebrows and a moustache.

Noticing the artwork on Ron's breakfast, Dad chuckled. "It's a bit too early for Movember, Ron. Are you planning to grow one this year?"

"One what? Oh a moustache." He laughed. "Maybe I will this year." Ron stroked his imaginary facial hair, pondering the idea. "To moustache, or not to moustache, that is the question." He tried to strike a thoughtful pose, with his fist supporting his chin.

Dad was pleasantly surprised. Even his son's humour was back; something he hadn't heard for the longest time. Taking a page from his son's book, he took the ketchup bottle and sprayed an image of a fish, giving it gills, fins, and eyes.

Ron knew Dad had once been an artist, having taken art lessons for several years as a child. Given how long it had been since he'd had those lessons, Ron was shocked at how good the fish looked, even though it was made with ketchup.

"Dear, would you stop wasting ketchup? We've been through two bottles already in less than a week!" Mom said.

"But, dear! I'm behind in my work and I need to ketch up." Smiling mischievously, Dad waited for Mom's judgement on his corny joke.

Ron just burst out laughing, drinking some water to stifle the chuckling.

Mom shook her ladle at Dad, indicating he was going to be in trouble if he kept this up. Dad slowly and solemnly put away the ketchup bottle, putting on a big frown and faking some tears. "I'm sorry, ketchup. My dear wife wants us to part. I shall miss squirting you ..."

Mom slapped her forehead, but realizing she had soap in her hand, she ended up getting bubbly soap all over her hair and head. Soon all three were laughing hilariously, both at Dad's mock sadness and Mom's mishap.

Outside in the garden, the birds busied themselves with eating all sorts of crawly creatures, oblivious to the outrageous laughter happening inside the house.

Still chuckling from breakfast, Ron drove to work, with good thoughts of Penny floating around in his head, reminding him of the precious time they'd had together. Gathering his work materials, Ron put them in a bag to keep them from getting wet in the rain as he walked into the office.

The weather had certainly changed in the fall, being wetter and colder than the balmy summer everyone enjoyed earlier.

With one hand holding an umbrella and the other hanging on to his work bag, Ron struggled in the wind and rain to keep balance while trying not to get wet. Arriving at the entrance, he shook everything like a dog, spraying water in all directions.

Seeing the security guard, Clyde, watching him, Ron smiled sheepishly and retracted his umbrella, glad to be out of the downpour.

"Morning, Clyde! I'm as wet as a dog," he said, laughing.

"Good morning, Ron! Just be careful, the floor is quite wet and slippery."

As if on cue, another worker rushing to clock in nearly slipped while running and just at the last second managed to regain her balance.

Tilting his head to the worker, Clyde chuckled. "See what I mean?"

Ron nodded in acknowledgement and walked slowly over the wet tiles until he was safely on the less threatening carpet. Looking curiously and cautiously at the cubicle in the corner, Ron checked to see if Walter had been let go yet. Not seeing anyone there, he quietly asked a neighbouring office worker if Walter was gone.

"He's gone. Boss fired him yesterday evening after you left. Good riddance, I'd say!"

Ron saluted the man, thanking him for the intel. After punching in with his card, Ron shed his wet coat and went to his desk to fire up the computer. As he was logging in, a familiar face appeared behind him.

"Guess where Greg and I went? Grouse Mountain! The trails were amazing, and we even saw several deer."

Ron was surprised at Rhonda's news. "Grouse Grind is a pretty tough hike. You and Greg hiked all the way up?"

A part of Ron was suspicious, given Rhonda and Greg were both fairly obese and not in the fittest shape.

"Of course not. We took the gondola."

Ron looked at Rhonda in the most criticizing way, as if to say they'd missed the best part of going to Grouse Mountain.

But throwing her a thumbs-up, he went over to the break room to get some coffee.

Going over to Garret's office, Ron spent the next few minutes getting up to date on what their department was doing and what analysis he needed to do today and for the coming week.

"The whole point of this cost-benefit analysis is to see if subsidized electricity rates would attract enough capital, investment, and jobs to BC, and especially northern BC, to make the subsidies worthwhile," Garret said. "If we can make investment in BC more attractive and increase economic development, we can improve the economy of BC, which is one of our primary objectives at BC Electric. So, do you think you can handle this project, Ron? You'll have several aides to help you crunch the numbers if needed."

"I'll take it. Thanks, Garret. Sounds exciting." Throwing a salute with his assignment folder, Ron walked back to his desk, feeling highly motivated to work as the caffeine and adrenaline kicked into his system. Looking at the list of aides available for his delegation of tasks, he decided to start with the workers Cliff and Pauline. But as Garret mentioned to him, it was very likely he would need every single one of his aides to help if he wanted to finish the project on time.

The first part of the project would involve identifying all benefits and social benefits to society in general, whether that be profits for firms or consumer surplus, which is the difference in value between what a consumer values a good for and what it will cost.

He decided to assign Cliff to the tally of all possible benefits to society, whereas Pauline would identify the multiplier effect of the benefits incurred.

Having emailed them and assigned their starting tasks, Ron went on to do some preliminary research on which industries relied heavily on cheap, reliable electricity, and what percentage of their total costs consisted of energy. Ron also started research into the cost of increasing the capacity of energy generation in the north, and costs of relocation for companies. The main industries in the north already taking advantage of the cheap electricity were aluminum manufacturers and lumber mills, given the large stock of trees available.

Ron also found out that the public's domestic demand for energy was flat, if not declining, as the population of the north was generally falling due to the effect known as the "brain drain." Another factor was that energy efficiency was becoming more mainstream in society, reducing electricity demand across BC.

Seeing a notification on his email, Ron was surprised to see Cliff had already found some preliminary results:

> Hi Ron,
>
> I've started tallying the benefits, starting with net producer surplus of existing industries if energy rates were to be lowered by 25%. The amount comes to $12.5 million a year saved by businesses and industries, while the cost of the discount in electricity is $6 million, resulting in a net social surplus of $6.5 million. But accounting for opportunity cost, if BC Electric had sold the electricity at the current rates, the difference in revenue would be exactly the amount of the net social surplus; $6.5 million but with a producer cost of an additional $12.5 million with a net social deficit of $6 million. I will get back to you with more results.
>
> Cliff

After reading the report, Ron made a mental note to recommend Cliff if any management positions were open; his efficiency and quality of work were both really impressive to Ron. After reading through Cliff's report, Ron started calculating the potential cost of providing adequate infrastructure to support development and industry in the north. Issues such as freeze-thaw, permafrost, and snowfall all posed challenges to setting up industry in northern BC. He would need to calculate these costs before even comparing the potential increases in net benefit to society. Ron realized that in addition to the infrastructure costs, setup costs, and costs of relocation, there were also the inevitable costs of global warming. He thought that while it may seem like higher temperatures in the north might be a good thing, actually, several problems might occur. The warming temperatures allowed more pine beetles to survive, resulting in huge groves of dead trees, a waiting fire hazard. Also, the higher temperatures increased erosion as permafrost melted and the land became more unstable.

Ron researched all these avenues, making sure to leave no stone unturned when it came to the costs of subsidized energy. A problem he kept encountering was the presence of conspiracy theories, unscientific claims, and skewed perspectives that kept popping up in his search results.

As a large entity under governmental scrutiny, BC Electric had to show responsibility in how it did its research and where it found its information.

Ron also recalled how his university professors abhorred online encyclopedias, treating them as abominable as the plague. Settling on information from Environment Canada, as well as several academic journals looking into the same topic of environmental costs, Ron's cost-benefit analysis was starting to come together. He then started calculating the benefits of substituting fossil fuels for clean hydroelectricity, but he soon found out it was as elusive as trying to hold on to water in his hand. The range in projected benefits of changing to electricity stretched from a low of zero to possibly a million dollars. Given all these costs, it became apparent that the most expensive cost would be building the infrastructure, followed by global warming effects on the region, and lastly, maintaining infrastructure in the long run.

Taking a pause, Ron suddenly remembered that he'd brought a picture from home for his desk. Looking in his bag, he carefully pulled out a picture frame and placed it on his desk: it was a portrait of him and Penny. They were in their badminton attire and were wielding rackets, with smiles as big as the sea. Touching the frame fondly, Ron smiled, forever remembering Penny as his girlfriend, his partner in life, and his joy.

Getting back to his work, he was concerned that Pauline still hadn't given him a preliminary report, despite having worked on it for several hours already. Walking over to her cubicle, Ron saw she was on her phone, apparently texting someone. She stopped when she heard Ron approaching.

"Oh, uh, Ron. I'm sorry. I'll get that report to you soon." She ended her sentence awkwardly.

Ron didn't even need to say anything. He simply warned her with a hand signal, shaking his finger to tell her to be more responsible.

Looking over at the clock, he realized it was almost lunchtime. So he headed over to the break room, where he had his lunch in the fridge.

Pretty soon there was a lineup at the microwave; the air smelled of fish, curry, and tomato sauce as everyone heated up their meals.

Suddenly the lights flickered, and the microwave beeped several times as it restarted. Everyone looked around and shrugged, not knowing what had happened.

Then the entire office began to shake, slowly at first, then getting more and more severe. People started screaming, while others dived under tables, desks, and other furniture to avoid tiles falling from the ceiling. Glass cups and ceramic plates fell out of the cupboards and shattered, littering the ground with broken shards.

Ron hurried to his desk and told others to hide like he was. "Get under cover, guys! Hurry!" he yelled. As he waved his hand, the rest of the employees scampered to whatever cover they could find, some opting to hide under the break room table.

Thanking his lucky stars, Ron was glad he was on the main floor of the office building; he could just imagine the terror of being on the top floor nearly ten stories above the ground. He winced as he heard the sound of windowpanes falling from upstairs, crashing down onto the ground.

Waiting for what seemed like an eternity, everyone remained sheltered, unsure of when the earthquake would be over and wary of aftershocks.

Ron shakily took out his phone and tried to call his parents, but all he heard was beeping as if the lines were busy; he was tremendously worried for his parents' safety.

"Is everyone okay? Guys? Shout out if you're alright" he called out.

"I'm fine, just a bit dusty."

"We're alright"

"I'm all good, Ron. Should we evacuate everyone now?" Rhonda asked shakily. Her voice had an element of fear in it.

"Yes, I think it's time to get everyone out," Ron said. "Okay, everyone. Don't panic. Calmly walk to the entrance leading to the parking lot, please. Stay calm, everyone."

Noticing everyone was stuck at the entrance and that no one was going out, Ron pushed to the front and realized the electric glass doors were out of service with the power out.

"Clyde, could you manually open the doors?"

"Afraid not, Ron. They're fully automatic with no manual switches. But I can use this metal stand to break through 'em. Is there any other way?"

Trying to manually force the doors open, Ron put his full weight behind them, but they still wouldn't budge. Pretty soon his arms and shoulders were sore from trying to wedge the doors open.

"You're right, Clyde. There's no way to force them open. You'll have to smash them in. Everyone back up, there's going to be lots of shattered glass, so back up, guys."

Clyde positioned himself and, taking the metal pole, used it like a ram to bash the door, cracking the glass on the first hit, but not making an opening. The second hit fractured it even more. Finally, on the third hit, the glass shattered and an opening was created so everyone could walk out to the foyer. They needed to break one more door to exit the glass office building.

Bang! Bang! Bang!

Clyde's rod broke through the final door, and people flooded through the opening into the safety of the parking lot. Huddled into little groups, they expressed mixed emotions of fear and relief that the worst was over.

Although the structure was damaged, the entire office staff suffered only a few scrapes and bruises, and everyone was otherwise safe and unhurt. A bunch of people were on their phones, trying to connect to loved ones.

"Is that everyone?" Ron asked. "Wait, where's Garret? Clyde, I think Garret is still inside!"

"We should go back inside to check," Clyde said. "Let's go, Ron."

Carefully they reentered the building and picked their way over the broken glass and around furniture strewn across the office floor. Heading over to Garret's office, they noticed a large bookshelf had fallen.

Quickly going in, fearing the worst, they found Garret pinned under the shelf.

"Garret! Garret! Are you alright! Garret! Can you hear me?" Clyde called.

"He's unconscious," Ron told him. "Help me get this shelf off him."

Together they moved the shelf and, seeing the bruising on Garret's side, realized that he was internally bleeding from being hit by the heavy piece of furniture. Realizing that picking up Garret might injure him more due to the unseen wound, they phoned emergency medical service to report the need for an ambulance for him.

Staying by Garret's side, they waited, and Ron tried again to contact his parents. This time the call went through, and he anxiously called out, "Mom? Dad? Are you guys okay? Is anyone hurt?"

"Ron! Thank goodness you're okay! We're fine, Dad's aquarium broke, but other than that, we're alright. Dad even managed to save the fish, so don't worry about us. But are you alright, Ron?"

"I'm fine, Mom. We're helping someone who's injured, but most of us are unhurt. Could you also call Penny's parents to see if they're okay too?"

"Okay, we will. Stay safe, Son. Alright?"

"I will, Mom, don't worry."

Focusing back on Garret, Ron was starting to get worried at how long the ambulance was taking. The bruising on Garret's side was getting larger and darker, spreading like darkness swallowing up the light.

"Clyde, we can't do anything. It's an internal injury. But I'm afraid if nothing else changes quickly, it's not going to end well. Can you find a first aid kit? I'll see if there's anything we can do to help."

Clyde headed towards the break room, where the first aid kit was held. Being careful not to step on the splattered food dropped everywhere, he opened the cupboard and found the kit. Taking it down, he hurried back to Ron, who was trying to wake Garret up.

"Clyde, stay with Garret. I'm going to let someone outside know where to direct the EMS paramedics when they come. I'll be back soon."

Rushing through the office, Ron stopped by his desk and recovered his picture of Penny, which was undamaged despite the earthquake.

Outside, he located the receptionist and told her that if the EMS personnel came, to direct them inside where Garret was waiting.

Dashing back inside, he knelt with Clyde beside Garret, feeling so helpless yet wanting to do something to help save him. Going through Garret's desk, Ron looked through several booklets and leaflets.

"What are you doing, Ron?" Clyde asked.

"Garret has a wife and kids; they should probably be notified of what happened to him. I'm looking for some emergency contact number."

Clyde took Garret's phone and handed it to Ron. "This might be easier. Look through his contacts."

Ron scrolled through the recent calls and noticed several were directed to Annie White. "Garret's last name is White, right?" Ron said. "I think I found his wife."

Calling Annie's number, Ron thought of how to tell her about Garret—about how to let her know.

"Hello, Garret?" a woman answered. "I've been trying to call you! Honey where are you? Are you alright?"

"Hi, Annie? This is Garret's coworker Ron. Are you Garret's wife?"

"Yes, that's me. Can you tell me what happened to my husband? Where is Garret?"

"Garret … He's unconscious right now in the office. He's also bleeding internally. We're doing what we can, but he needs to get to a hospital. I'm afraid, though, it might be a while before EMS has time to pick him up because of the earthquake. I'm sorry ..." Through the phone, Ron could hear an infant crying in the background. "I'll let you know which hospital he'll go to once the paramedics come. We'll try our best to save him, okay?"

"Thank you, Ron. Please let us know which hospital he'll be in when you find that out," Annie said.

A couple of minutes later, they could hear the sirens of the ambulance and the rushing in of paramedics.

"Over here, please!" Ron called out. "Thank you for coming so quickly! He has internal bleeding on his side. Please be careful!"

Carrying in a stretcher while avoiding all the furniture strewn about, the paramedics carefully loaded Garret onto the stretcher and carted him away.

"Oh, by the way, which hospital will he be taken to?" Ron asked. "The family wants to see him, and I can direct them to whichever hospital he will go to."

"The closest hospital is Burnaby Green Timbers," one of the paramedics replied. "Tell the family he'll be transported there. He'll likely be in the ICU, given the seriousness of the injury."

Climbing out of the wreckage of the building, Ron and Clyde arrived back in the parking lot, where everyone was gathered The crowd, seeing the pair, broke out in applause for their heroic efforts.

Acknowledging the gratitude, the two men sat down to rest, contemplating what had just happened.

Asking around, they found out several others had also been injured, but thankfully Garret was the only serious case.

Driving home was a nightmare. Besides the occasional pothole, vehicle crash, or fallen tree, there were hundreds if not thousands of cars trying to get home after the earthquake. Turning on the radio, Ron listened to the devastating situation Vancouver was in as a result of the disaster.

"Scientists have measured the quake at a magnitude 8.3 on the Richter scale, the biggest in the Metro Vancouver region for years," the announcer said. "We have reports of multiple older buildings collapsing, but due to stringent building requirements, most modern structures suffered only minor damage. Several dozen car crashes were reported, along with fallen trees knocking down power lines and leaving millions in the dark. Authorities are reminding the public to have emergency supplies to last seventy-two hours before expecting help to arrive. Probably the worst-hit area was Richmond, where the dykes were severely damaged and seawater flooded coastal areas of the city. Liquefaction also damaged hundreds of buildings in Richmond and parts of Surrey that were built on loose ground material."

After several hours of inching along in traffic, Ron finally arrived home and, noticing that the garage door sensor light didn't turn on, he figured the power was out.

When he entered the house, he found Dad sweeping up glass from the broken aquarium, while Mom was soaking up the wet carpet with paper towels.

Looking up from his cleaning, Dad warned Ron, "Hey, watch out for glass. I still need to sweep the rest of the floor. What a mess! I mean, look at my aquarium! It's a disaster. Were you guys fine at the office?"

"My manager, Garret, suffered an injury and is in hospital for internal bleeding. I just called his wife, and he has two kids. I don't know if he'll survive."

Dad patted Ron on the back, consoling him as he had always done for his son.

"It's just, his wife and kids seem so worried," Ron said "I just hope that Garret's okay." Wiping away a tear, he smiled and took a brush to help clean up the glass as Dad put a hand on his shoulder. "I'm fine, Dad, thanks. Let's clear everything out so we can have some decent dinner at least."

Mom frowned. "Sorry to disappoint, Ron, but the natural gas is off, as is the electricity. So there's no way to cook until the utilities are back and working."

"How about Dad's propane stove? The one we use for camping trips?" Ron wasn't willing to give up on a hot meal even after an earthquake.

"Now that's the best idea you've had all day, Son," Dad said. "I'll go get it prepped for later. But let's clean up this mess first, agreed?"

"Yes, sir! But if your aquarium is broken, where are your fish, Dad?"

Dad simply pointed to several jars on the kitchen island. "Unfortunately, they have to stay in those jars till I can find another aquarium. Your mother nearly took my head off for using her tomato sauce jars for the fish."

Mom busied herself preparing for the camping meal, not even trying to remember their argument. "Honey," she said, "don't forget the stove has to be used outside. Otherwise there'll be too much smoke. I've heard of families getting sick from the fumes."

Dad nodded in agreement. "I'll volunteer to cook outside while you two stay nice and warm indoors. The things I do for my family. I must be the best man there is."

Mom and Ron started laughing at Dad's self-praise. "How very humble of you," Ron said.

Dad kept praising himself. "I'm a handsome husband, devoted parent, caring counsellor—"

"Stop, Dad. Please, Dad, stop!" Ron said. He and Mom were holding their sides from the burst of laughter bubbling up, and they laughed till their sides ached.

Continuing the cleaning, Ron tried to turn on the TV, but

it wasn't a surprise that it didn't turn on, given the power outage.

"So where were you guys when the shaking began?" he asked. "Did you take cover?" Ron started cutting vegetables and meat for the stove.

"Your mom and I were watching TV, actually, when I noticed the ceiling fan was shaking. Pretty soon the whole house was shaking, and that's when the tank cracked and all the aquarium water gushed out. I spent the next fifteen minutes saving all my poor fish."

Mom shook her head, lamenting. "Your father cared so much about his fish, he didn't even ask if I was alright from the earthquake!"

Dad put on an injured expression and grabbed hold of Mom's hand as he lamented as well. "Oh my goodness, is that an injury on your finger, dear? I am so sorry I didn't inquire about your health, my dear! Here, let me make that injury get better." Dad then repetitively kissed Mom's finger, and she grew red with embarrassment yet again.

Ron shook his head. "I'd hate to interrupt your romantic escapade, but there's a poor hungry boy out here waiting for his meal."

Mom smiled mischievously. "Oh dear, we have a hungry dog begging for food. Shall we toss him a few bones and scraps?"

Dad caught the drift and did one better. "I think this doggy should work for his dinner. If he can help me move the fish to the living room, we'll let him eat a proper dinner."

Ron rolled his eyes at his parents' theatrics. Then he looked at the fish in the jars, swimming in their confined spaces. "When did you get this orange one, Dad?"

Dad looked at the fish Ron was gesturing towards. "It's a clown loach. Your grandfather's favourite tropical fish, the only one he ever bought. He's a feisty one."

"The stripes look like a zebra, but with orange."

Picking up several jars, Ron helped Dad move them to the living room table.

All the fish were in jars of the same size, and he felt sorry for the bigger fish that could barely swim around in the tiny containers. The smaller fish fared better but were crammed with four or five others who were in the same predicament.

Thanking Ron for the help, Dad went to the garage to find the propane stove, while Mom continued prepping the vegetables and meats to be cooked. Although there were the usual Asian vegetables, beef tenderloin, and chicken thighs, one key element of dinner was missing: rice. Mom was also cooking two kinds of meat in hopes of not wasting any meat to spoilage, since the fridge was not working due to the power outage.

"I found it, dear! You'll never guess where we stored it. Next to the lawnmower." Dad proudly walked in with the stove in one hand and a propane tank in the other. Taking it all outside to the deck, he attached the tank to the stove and tried to start the flame.

Clink! Clink! Clink!

The flame didn't ignite, and while the hiss of gas continued, Dad kept trying to light it, until finally a huge ball of fire ignited in a surprising mini explosion. Even Dad was forced back a few paces to avoid getting singed, but the stove was now ready. He took the food from Mom and started cooking the meat first in a cast-iron skillet. The moment the meat touched the pan, a satisfying sizzling sound started as it began to sear, sealing in the juices. Using a brush, Dad added the marinade to the meat, a sweet and salty sauce Mom always made. Dad sautéed the broccoli, celery, and bell peppers in a nonstick pan next to the meat. He poured some of the melted fat from the meat onto the vegetables, making them shiny and glimmering in the light.

Although Dad cooked only occasionally, he was, in fact, a better cook than Mom. But he often let Mom rule the kitchen as her domain, helping out only once in a while.

Having seared the chicken thighs so that the skin was crispy, he flipped them over to finish cooking. The beef would take a bit longer to cook, given the thickness of the tenderloin. Dad had opted to cook the whole tenderloin instead of slicing it into pieces. This way the juices would make the meat moist instead of dry as sawdust. After finishing the chicken, Dad gave everyone a piece and drizzled some of the marinade over the perfectly crisp skin. Using a large spoon, he divided up the vegetables for everyone while waiting patiently for the tenderloin to cook.

While they waited for the beef, the family started eating, so as not to let the cooked food grow cold. The thighs were crispy outside and juicy inside, and the vegetables were cooked just right—slightly soft yet still with some crunchiness and not completely mushy.

Ron enjoyed the dinner with gusto, almost forgetting the dire circumstance they were in post-earthquake. He took the broccoli and soaked the floret in the juices and sauce, then ate it promptly, relishing the taste.

Dad paused his eating to check on the beef, and, giving a thumbs-up, he signalled that it had finished cooking. Taking the tenderloin off the pan and putting it on a cutting board, he sliced it into small fillets, serving them with the sauce made from the drippings and marinade. The meat was cooked a perfect medium-rare, and everyone was soon savouring the melt-in-your-mouth beef.

"Ron, would you like to tag along with me Tuesday to watch how I manage my business?" Dad asked. "I'm doing an emergency routine check to make sure all departments are working properly after the quake. You game?"

Ron looked up and finished chewing before replying.

"Yeah, that's a great idea! Sure, I'll come along. We're all on leave while the office is being cleaned up. I've always wondered what your company does. It'd be cool."

"I remember when your father showed me what he did for a living; he was trying to impress me so that I would accept his proposal."

"And look where I am now, my dear. Apparently it worked! I caught the best wife of all!" Dad quickly planted another wet kiss on Mom's cheek before she could retaliate to his not-so-humble attitude.

Helping clear out the dishes, Ron was quite surprised at how well the camping stove had worked. Dad unhooked the propane. Shaking it, he confirmed there was still enough for another meal.

After everything was cleaned, Ron went upstairs, excited to go along with Dad on his supervising site review—a rare opportunity to see the company his dad had built from the ground up.

Checking his phone for messages, he noticed there were several that had not been read, and he noticed that almost all of them were from Garret's wife, Annie.

Hello Ron,

I've tried calling you but I kept getting sent to voicemail, so I'm going to try texting you. I just wanted to thank you for going back into the office to be with and save Garret. You and Clyde gave Garret a fighting chance, despite being so injured. I just wanted to update you on Garret; he's not doing too well, but he's hanging in there. If there's any change, we'll let you know.

Annie

Scrolling up to the latest text sent nearly two hours later, Ron realized something terrible had happened.

Ron,

I've got bad news about Garret. He succumbed to his injuries just now. Even though we couldn't save him, we are grateful for what you and Clyde did. We are going to plan a funeral in a few days or weeks, and it would be nice if you could come. Garret would have wanted to say goodbye.

Yours, Annie

Ron was astonished. He could identify with Annie's pain of losing someone she cared about, and he knew the best thing to do was to just be there for her and her kids, crying with them or even just sitting with them in silence. When he lost Penny, it felt the worst when the people around him were openly happy—just as how salt stings a wound.

Taking his car keys, Ron rushed downstairs to where his parents were chatting, obviously sorely missing the TV.

"Honey, a forty-gallon tank is nothing. I say we get an eighty-gallon tank and the matching stand, of course. Trust me, it will look awesome when I'm done with it," Dad said.

"I don't want to argue, dear, but with a tank that big, what will happen if we have another earthquake? The whole house will be under a foot of water!"

"Earthquakes in BC over six in magnitude are one in ten years or even longer, and if we get a better stand, there's less likelihood of the tank shattering. Trust me, honey, I've done my homework."

"You know I trust you, dear. I just want to be careful. Fine, fine, I'll agree, an eighty-gallon tank it is." Then she turned around and said, "Oh, Ron. Did you have a good rest?"

Dad also turned around to see Ron coming down the stairs.

"I just found out my manager passed away. I'm going to visit Annie, his widow, at the hospital. I tried my best to save him. It just wasn't enough. I just hope I can help Annie as everyone helped me when I lost Penny."

"You're doing the right thing, Ron. I'm glad you're moving on and even helping someone else in need. We're proud of you, Son." Dad got up and patted him on the back, then he and Mom watched as Ron went out.

Arriving at the hospital, Ron recalled Mom's warning to wear a mask. Going inside, he asked where the family rooms were so he could find Annie and her kids. As he walked through the mass of people coming in and out, the bustle of the crowd was quite unnerving, as social distancing was not always possible. Having texted Annie beforehand, he knew that she would be waiting for him and that they would meet up in one of the family rooms. Ron headed to the miniature rooms and found her holding her baby.

"Annie? Hi, it's Ron. I got your texts. I'm so terribly sorry for your loss."

Annie nodded her head in acknowledgement but put a finger to her mouth, gesturing at her sleeping toddler. Speaking in a whisper, she said, "He was up all evening saying goodbye to Papa. I'm going to let him rest a bit before going home. You're welcome to stay if you'd like. I'll warn you, though, that sofa is so comfortable you won't want to leave once you've sat down on it."

Smiling, Ron chose to sit on the armchair, fondly watching the toddler, who was drooling onto his bib.

"He looks like his father," Ron said. "Same blue eyes, small ears. He even has the same chin."

Annie smiled as well. "You're right. When we looked at childhood pictures of Garret, they're like twins. Like father, like son."

"How old is the younger one? He looks about one to me."

"Little Denver here is fourteen months. We just weaned him off milk nearly seven months ago. You should see him tackle his applesauce. He eats it like he's facing a famine. We're trying to get him to eat more vegetables though. He only seems to like carrot and peas."

Shaking his head, Ron could relate to the toddler's pickiness. "My dad didn't like peas since he was a kid. Even now he won't eat peas unless they're in a pod. Occasionally Mom makes him eat a spoonful of them—citing the need for protein, but it's pretty funny watching Dad gag while trying to swallow it."

"Nope, my baby just really likes his peas. Mashed of course, as he can't chew yet, and we wanted to prevent any choking hazard. My firstborn was far pickier. He would eat only spinach—no carrot, no peas, no apple, no broccoli. It was a struggle for me and Garret."

"You should probably head on home. It's getting dark earlier these days," Ron said. "Do you need help carrying the tiny Garret to the car? He can keep sleeping that way."

"Are you sure? I don't want to be a burden. Thank you so much, Ron."

Gently lifting the toddler to his shoulder, Ron draped him in a blanket and followed Annie out of the room. "What is this little guy's name, by the way?"

"Oh, that's Ricardo. Garret had just finished watching a Latino movie, and he wanted to name his kid after the main character."

"My father was almost named Antonio. It's interesting how Spanish names are quite popular nowadays. Oh, your little man is drooling quite a bit," Ron said, laughing.

Annie was extremely embarrassed, and she fussed over her toddler. "I'm so sorry, Ron! Here, we're almost at the car. Oh, Ricardo, you drooling monster!"

She hurriedly put the baby into the car seat. Then she relieved Ron of her toddler and put him into a second car seat. Giving Ron some tissue, she apologized for her toddler's drool.

"One time, Garret was carrying Ricardo back from preschool in winter, and he drooled all over Garret's sweater. The worst of it was that the drool froze in the cold air, and Garret was like an icicle when we arrived home." Pausing awkwardly as Annie thought back to her memories with Garret, Ron held his silence, knowing now was not the time to be overly talkative.

Putting Ricardo's blanket back on the sleeping child, Ron gently closed the back door.

"Well, if you ever need anything, Annie, don't be afraid to ask. I'm here to help. I can be a shoulder for you to lean on. Just not drool on," he said with a laugh.

Smiling a little, Annie hugged Ron and thanked him for his help. "Well, we'll see you next time. Thanks again."

Ron went back to his parked car and dabbed at the drool on his coat. He smiled, thinking of little Ricardo's restful sleep and wondered what little dreams he would dream of. He drove back home, hoping the power would be back by the time he arrived at the house and hoping that Annie and her family would be alright.

Arriving home, he was disappointed that the garage light was still off, but honestly, he wasn't surprised given the severity of the earthquake. The news on the radio had estimated that roughly a hundred people had died and thousands injured.

As he quietly closed the door, there was an eerie silence in the home. It was unlike Mom and Dad to be sleeping this early. Seeing a note on the countertop, Ron realized his parents were out.

Ron,

Dad and I are going out to visit a friend, We'll be back at

around ten. There are egg tarts in the fridge if you want some. Don't leave the fridge open too long, we're trying to conserve the cold air with the power out.

P.S. Your dad ate all the Portuguese tarts, so only the regular ones are left!

Opening the fridge, Ron snatched the tarts quickly and closed the door in a millisecond, happily munching away at the sweet dessert. He remembered the time Dad made egg tarts almost from scratch, buying the shells and mixing eggs with sweetened condensed milk. He then baked them in the oven till they were perfectly custardy and silky smooth with a crusty exterior.

Going upstairs, he began to wonder how long it would be before work would start again and life would get back to normal. Not only had COVID-19 stopped most social gatherings, but the earthquake had also damaged much of the metropolitan region's utility infrastructure, making normal work impossible in the near term.

After cleaning up in the bathroom, Ron lay down on his bed, wanting to check his email but realized the router was offline. As he drifted off to sleep, a familiar dream came back. In his mind's eye, he saw Penny and her two kids. But then the picture started to blur. When it refocused, Ron found himself looking at Annie and her two infants, then the image faded away.

When Ron woke up several hours later, he couldn't remember the details of the dream—only that it was somehow important. Sitting on his bed and trying to recall the dream, he couldn't help but smell the aroma of cooking eggs and bacon, and the brewing of coffee. The electricity and gas were back on. Lured by his hunger and need for caffeine, Ron quickly washed up and walked down the stairs.

"Hey, Dad! Today's the day, right? We're going to tour

your company's operations?" Ron's eyes were wide open, and he was excited to learn about what his father actually did for a living—what he had started as a young man and now oversaw as a hands-off owner.

"Breakfast first, Ron. Sit. We'll get going soon enough."

"Your father's right," Mom said. "You need energy for the day. Here, have some toast, eggs, and bacon. Sausage is on the way."

As Ron helped himself to the delicious breakfast-blend coffee, Dad warned him about the effects of caffeine. "Careful you don't drink too much coffee. You'll be looking for the washroom half the time while we're out working."

Heeding his father's warning, Ron took only sips of the coffee, feeling a slight buzz from the caffeine. Dad continued eating his omelet, once again drowned in ketchup to Mom's disapproval.

"Here's some sausage, Ron," Mom said.

"Dear, this omelet is delicious! It's exceptionally tasty today. What different recipe did you use?" Dad asked.

Mom smiled mischievously. "Oh, it was nothing. Just a little bacon fat."

Dad froze, with a morsel of egg halfway to his mouth as he realized he had eaten his forbidden food. His fearful expression turned into resentment as he realized Mom was joking.

She laughed. "Dear, I was only joking! I used butter instead of oil. You should have seen your face, honey!"

"Your mother can be so cruel at times," Dad said to Ron.

Mom went over to Dad and started ruffling his hair in affection. "I'm sorry, dear. I'll try to be more sensitive next time."

Holding Mom's hand, Dad patted it in thanks for her willingness to adapt. "Thanks, honey. It means a lot to me that you listen to me. Truly it does."

Mom then hugged Dad, both glad that the impromptu joke was over and both were willing to move on and learn from the mishap. Ron looked at them both with admiration. One of the reasons Dad married Mom was that she was willing to respect him and trust him to lead the family. On the other hand, Mom looked up to Dad because of his wealth of knowledge and willingness to protect and provide for her. Both had troubles and arguments that needed to be resolved from time to time, and when they did fix their conflicts, they grew stronger, closer, and more affectionate with one another.

After finishing up breakfast, Mom said goodbye to the boys as they left in Dad's pickup truck, off to start Dad's routine check of company operations. They drove for about fifteen minutes, eventually arriving at the office of Lifetime Supply Delivery, or LSD, which was the company Dad founded.

"Hello, Mr. Lee. How are you, sir?" the receptionist said. Ron noticed she seemed quite nervous, probably because Dad was the big boss.

"I'm fine," Dad replied. "We're just going to take a look around to see if the earthquake hindered any of our operations, so don't mind us. Oh, and this is my son, Ron. I'll be showing him the ropes of what goes on every day."

Nodding, the receptionist went back to being preoccupied with work, not wanting to seem like she was wasting company time.

Dad then walked over to the registration department, where people set up their lifetime supplies of anything, from vegetables to office supplies.

"So, Ron, what happens here is that people weigh the benefits and costs of investing with us, as we offer them a lifetime of supplies, while they provide us with an initial investment to help pay for the supplies and provide a yield in the interest rate, which goes to the company. We calculate the required investment by finding out the minimum principal investment needed to earn enough to pay for all the supplies, pay our company, and adjust for inflation. The beauty of this system is that the investments provide a return in perpetuity, meaning the children and grandchildren of these investors will benefit from the continuous delivery of supplies. That way, vertical equity is achieved, as the future generations are taken care of just as well as the generation today. It is modelled after the fund in Alaska, which provides perpetual payments to all Alaskans from investments made using the royalties from fossil fuel revenues. Interesting, isn't it?"

"Yeah, I think you've taken the concept of long-run sustainability and built a company on it. I mean, it's responsible, frugal, and innovative. Quite amazing, Dad. Quite amazing."

Entering the second department, Ron noticed there were only computer stations there—and piles of papers on each desk.

"This is the order and shipping department, where we handle all the shipping needed to serve previous investors as well as newly registered members," Dad said. "We have to be very careful to make sure every order is fulfilled and on time, otherwise, our brand may suffer. People rely on our deliveries for everything from basic cooking to important meetings and conferences."

Picking up a clipboard at the front, Dad scanned the numbers, explaining at the same time to Ron what was being tallied.

"See this number here, 29,351? That's the number of people who have subscribed to our delivery service and made an initial investment to attain that status. So, the amount invested is nearly $150 million, resulting in roughly

$5 to $7 million in revenue, depending on the return on the investments."

Ron noticed a smaller number next to the initial number Dad pointed to. "What's that number, Dad?"

"That's the number of investors who cancelled their orders and got their full investment back. It's a good indicator of how well our customers trust our brand. You can see it's only a handful right now, so that's good. Since we invest only people's initial investment, we don't lose money by refunding their full amount. And when people see they can get a full refund anytime, it builds trust as well."

They moved on to the next area of the company. "The next department is our investment portfolio division, consisting of seven members who constantly manage our investments to make sure they're reliable, conservative, and stable while aiming for the highest yield possible with minimum risk."

Picking up and looking at a similar clipboard, Dad was pleasantly surprised. "Our rate of return, year to date, is roughly 9.5 percent. Not bad, considering the effect of COVID-19 right now on businesses. We try to keep a large portion of our investments in government bonds, which are much more stable than stocks, but with a lower yield. The final department is the customer service section. Any problems, conflicts, delays, and such are handled here, with our skilled CSAs. Each one of them handles roughly twenty to forty cases in a typical day. We have people speaking Punjabi, Hindi, French, Mandarin and even Tagalog."

Walking to the office spaces, Dad knocked on the CEO's door, and cautioned his son. "Now, be on your best behaviour. We're going to meet the top working man in the company."

Taking the advice, Ron straightened up his posture and stood as tall as he could as they entered.

"Mr. Lee, it's nice to see you," the man inside said. "And is this your son? He looks strong—not to mention he has your good looks." The CEO slyly winked at Dad, trying to flatter the usually serious man.

Dad laughed. "You're a flatterer, Jason. Yes, this is my son, Ron. He's somewhat of a fitness addict, not to mention he's a finance manager at BC Electric."

"So, you're from BC Electric, eh?" Jason said. "Your company took forever to restore power. We had to suspend work until the power came back on just this morning."

"I'm sorry, sir, but honestly that's not my department. I'm a business analyst, not a repair engineer. But I do understand the frustration of waiting for the power to come back."

"Quite impressive, yes. Would you mind if your father and I chatted a bit in private? We just have to discuss some corporate issues that have arisen. Thanks, bud!"

Ron walked out of the office and explored one of the office areas. He was astonished to see Annie fussing over some drawers in her cubicle. She was busy looking for something when he interrupted her to say hi.

"Hey, Annie! I didn't know you worked at my dad's company! You're back to work already? You should have applied for some time off with Garret, uh, being gone."

Annie was just as surprised to see Ron at her workplace. "Ron! I left my glasses here when I scrambled to go to the hospital, and I just came by to pick them up. So, wait a minute. Your father is Mr. Lee? As in the Mr. Lee who owns the company?"

"Yes, ma'am. That's me, Ron Lee. But this is actually the first time Dad has brought me to see the company."

Several employees looked over their cubicles to catch a glimpse of the athletically built Ron talking to Annie, gossiping among themselves at how she knew the owner's son.

"Ron, Ron! We're all done. Are you ready to go?" Dad emerged from the office hallway with the CEO.

"Alright, Annie. I gotta go. Catch you later? Say hi to Denver and Ricardo for me."

Giving a thumbs-up, she went back to searching for her glasses.

As Dad drove back home, he picked up on something between Ron and that girl. "Ron, are you friends with that girl? You two seemed like you know each other."

"Yeah, we barely know one another, but that was Garret's widow, the one I went to visit yesterday at the hospital. I didn't know she worked at your company. She was quite shocked to know I was your son. Are you some sort of celebrity, Dad?" Ron asked with a laugh.

"Nope, I just own 100 percent of the company's shares, so most people in the company know about me as the owner and founder. But I've pretty much retired to an occasional supervisory position, leaving all the big decisions to the CEOs and other management staff. That way I get to spend more time with your mother."

"Wait, so if you're not working, who pays for all our bills? Unless you sold some of your share in the company?"

"Nope, I saved up enough while I ran the company as a sole proprietorship, enough to retire on the interest gained from my investments. Also, your mother contributes with her sale of arts and crafts—don't sneeze at how much she earns. Just a word of advice, Ron: be careful when trusting people who know you're my son. Some people will do anything to move up the ranks of a company."

Digesting the informative warning from his dad, Ron was happy to see Annie doing fairly well—despite her loss. He thought back to the sleeping Ricardo and baby Denver, two vulnerable children who had forever lost their father. He thought perhaps there was some way for him to help them.

When they arrived back home, the dining room smelled of baking garlic bread, as well as fish, Dad's favourite protein by far. In the kitchen, several pots and pans were on the stove, bubbling and sizzling with delightful aromas.

The first thing Ron did was head upstairs and check his emails. There were several from BC Electric telling them work was resuming the next day. Likewise, Coach Lucas was restarting practice on the same day. What caught Ron's eye though was the most recent email, from Annie.

Hello Ron,

It was nice to see you today at work, and I never got to fully thank you for helping carry Ricardo to the car from the hospital. I've set Garret's funeral to be tomorrow at six in the evening. The service will be at the cemetery in the Fleetwood area. If you can come, I would really appreciate it.

You're a real friend, Ron, to both Garret and me as well.

In gratitude,

Annie

Sending a reply to the email to confirm his attendance, Ron struggled to word his sympathy:

Dear Annie,

You are very welcome, there's no need to thank me. It was my duty to help Garret, and I'm sure others would have done the same in my position. Thank you for your invitation, and I will attend Garret's funeral tomorrow at six.

P.S. If you need a shoulder to lean on during the service, let me know. I have two.

Yours,

Ron

After setting a reminder on his phone to attend the

funeral, Ron once again bounded downstairs to not miss dinner, which Mom and Dad were quickly finishing. Smelling the steaming dishes with aromas wafting through the air, Ron found himself nearly drooling, and he caught himself, slurping up his saliva before it dripped. Fortunately, his mom and dad both were too busy to notice, and Ron wiped the side of his mouth with his sleeve.

On the menu was Chinese broccoli, or *gie lan,* as well as a yellow leafy vegetable called *sui choi,* which was served with shiitake mushrooms and a savoury soy sauce. The main course was a previously frozen tilapia surrounded by *bok choi* and in a sweeter dark soy sauce, garnished by sautéed garlic and green onions. Lastly, there were string beans coated with olive oil and cooked with freshly minced garlic.

"You know, tilapia was your father's favourite fish in his childhood until your grandma switched to mostly salmon and trout," Mom said, smiling at Dad's eagerness to eat the fish dish.

Shaking his head, Dad lamented over his mother's strict dietary rules. "Those were sad days, all for the sake of preventing mercury poisoning. Large fish and bottom-feeding fish were strictly off the menu. No halibut, and no tilapia as well."

Ron took a huge bite out of a shiitake mushroom, enjoying the umami flavour and thick, savoury sauce. By the time he had eaten the mushroom, he had also finished his first bowl of rice and politely asked Mom for another.

"Eat more of the vegetables and meat; if you can't finish the rice, it's okay." Mom picked a good, hearty portion of fish and some *bok choi* and gently put it into Ron's bowl.

"Thanks, Mom," Ron said, then he went straight to chowing down on the food in his bowl. He agreed with Dad that the fish was very delicious.

Mom also took another piece of fish and gave it to Dad, who was very grateful his wife thought of him too.

"Thank you, dear. It's nice that you care about your poor, old husband too." Dad made the most innocent eyes that he could, looking at Mom and making her blush yet again. She then kept piling food onto his bowl until his rice was hidden under a layer of fish, vegetables, and mushrooms.

Ron shook his head at the pair and focused on tackling his own portion, nearly finishing the second bowl of rice and opting for another morsel of fish instead of the remaining rice. Once again, Dad gave one of the cheeks, or *meen gun*, to Mom, surprising even her.

Leaving the two hopeless romantics, Ron started cleaning up the dishes, giving his parents some space while they shamelessly flirted with one another.

As he was rinsing the dishes, Ron wondered what work would be like the next day without Garret in the office. It would be indeed hard to work without him there—at least without remembering him. He glanced over at Mom and Dad, who were chatting and chuckling like a pair of chipmunks.

After a while, his parents helped with clearing the table as well, bringing the plates to the sink.

"My, my, who's this good little man helping clean up the dishes?" Mom asked.

Ron played along. "I don't know, but he sure was taught well by his parents to help clean up."

Dad ignored the sarcasm and ruined the whole façade. "Thanks, Ron, for helping. Your mom and I were just chatting. We appreciate your help a lot."

"Honey! You ruined our game …" Mom said.

"I'm sorry, but sarcasm isn't in my repertoire of skills. I know, we can play a game where we multiply large numbers in our heads! It'll be fun. Come on!"

Ron hurried to finish the dishes, desperately trying not to get caught up in one of Dad's boring math games.

"Okay, so let's start with an easy one. What's thirty-two times thirty-three? Ron?"

With a look of injured pride, Dad watched as his son plugged his ears and ran back upstairs to his room. "That's fine, we'll play ourselves, then. Dear? Dear?" He was even more crestfallen as Mom also walked away, leaving him to finish the dishes and play his math game by himself.

Muttering to himself in his disappointment, Dad murmured that they were spoilsports and didn't know a good game even when they heard one.

Ron lay on his bed, thinking of Annie and wondering how he could help her and her children through their difficult time. He then remembered he would need to dress for the funeral the next day.

Picking out a black suit and pants, he carefully folded them into his bag, along with his gym clothes.

He took the bag to work in the morning and started his shift like any other, greeting Clyde the security guard and Rhonda. But something was different—something in his regimen of work. He went over to Garret's old office and found it locked with a note posted on the door:

> Our condolences to Garret White and his family.
>
> To all employees, the manager covering Garret's position will be Terry. Please bring any questions or requests to him on the second floor. Also please see him for your daily assignments as well.

He took one last look at the office, which was refurbished and reorganized. But in Ron's mind, he could still see Garret pinned under the bookshelf, unresponsive and in dire need of help. Turning around, he found himself facing a tall Black man who resembled a Hollywood movie star.

"Hello, are you Ron, the finance manager? My name's Terry, supervisory manager on the second floor," the man said.

"That would be me," Ron said. "Thanks for coming down. It saved me a trip going upstairs, although I could use the exercise." Ron laughed.

"You probably get enough exercise, by the looks of it," Terry said, alluding to Ron's toned body and muscular build. "My wife keeps telling me to work out, but I find it tremendously difficult to commit to an exercise schedule. It's all in the mind, I tell you. If you commit, you win it."

Ron smiled at the slogan. "That's pretty good. You're right, though. It does take quite a bit of work."

"Hard work, determination, and ambition are all powerful motives. They can almost guarantee success."

Ron raised an eyebrow "Almost?" he asked.

"Well, there's also the element of luck or accidental success, like how we invented penicillin with dirty petri dishes. Or the invention of Viag—"

Ron's work phone started ringing, so he nodded to Terry before sitting down and getting to work, eager to leave the conversation.

That workday was the slowest one Ron had ever experienced. Every time he looked at the clock, he thought the hand was moving in extra slow motion. The more he checked the time, the more it seemed barely any time had passed.

"You know, the more you stare at the clock, each second passes twice as slow."

Ron sat bolt upright, "Uh, Rhonda, I was just … Okay, okay, I was checking the clock. I just have something on my mind."

Rhonda nodded. "Is it about Garret? Trust me, he's on everyone's mind right now. He was one of the best managers this company has ever had. No one can ever replace him, in my mind at least."

Ron agreed with his coworker. "The office just isn't the same without him. Whoever the new guy is, he's going to have some big shoes to fill. I just hope it's someone as great as Garret. But whoever it may be, it's just going to be nice to go back to some form of normalcy. It's been a hectic year for all of us. First COVID-19, and now an earthquake. Whatever will come next?" Ron asked.

Rhonda raised an eyebrow. "How about a shark in a tornado? Killer birds? Zombies?"

Ron shook his head disapprovingly. "You're going to give me nightmares if you keep that up, Rhonda. I have enough fears in my mind. There's no need to add any more, thank you very much."

"Well, someone doesn't appreciate horror films. How could you not like killer birds? Pecking your eyes out, dive-bombing, and cracking open skul—"

Ron stood up and ushered Rhonda away from his cubicle. "Begone, you nuisance. Shoo! Shoo! Go plague someone else with your nonsense!" he said, laughing.

Stifling more laughter, he sat back down and tried to refocus on his work, but he couldn't do it without intrusive thoughts of murderous birds attacking him.

Heading to the copier, he remembered the incident with Walter, when he'd hijacked the printer, printing hundreds of pages of manuals. Garret had made the right decision in letting him go. There was no room in a workplace for malice and sabotage.

Punching out at the end of his shift, which seemed like it took forever to come, Ron said bye to Clyde one last time before heading to his car and driving to badminton practice.

As he merged into the highway, Ron noticed a small car had been following him since leaving the parking lot. When he merged into the fast lane, the car behind him did likewise. Trying not to panic, he kept driving till he finally passed a yellow light, forcing the car behind him to stop. Relieved that he was no longer being followed, Ron headed to the badminton gym, unnerved by the scary situation.

Changing into his gym clothes, Ron shared his scary situation with his buddies.

"That's pretty messed up, Ron. Why would anyone follow you? Do you think it might be a stalker?" Xu asked.

"Xu, why would anyone stalk someone as strong and well-built as Ron? Don't people usually stalk weak, defenceless victims to take advantage of?" Lucy asked as she shook her head.

"Maybe it's a psycho lady who's smitten by his build and good looks? Or perhaps a madwoman seeking a—" said Steve.

"Steve! You guys aren't making this any better. Psycho lady? Madwoman? Seriously?" Ron shook his head and walked onto the court, eager to change the subject.

"I was going to say trophy husband," Steve called after him. "You don't need to bite my head off."

Coach Lucas blew the whistle, and everyone got on the courts to start their training. First, everyone had to warm up, as stretching is the best way to prevent sprains and other injuries.

Once again, Ron was pitted against Lucy, the only other singles player on the team. She had some strapping on her left ankle after she suffering a slight sprain from an accident during the quake. Ron kept a mental note to not make her run too much so as not to put too much pressure on her injured foot.

Starting with a high service to the back of the line, he

crouched slightly to prepare for a potential smash. Lucy, instead of smashing it, cleared it to the back of Ron's court, forcing him to go back. Ron then tried slicing the birdie at a sharp angle to drop it in the front, cross-court near the net. Lucy tried to hit the birdie but wasn't there in time, as the birdie hit the ground, giving a point to Ron.

They continued trading shots till they were both quite tired yet still trying their best to hit winning shots. Ron's strategy was focused more on utilizing his strength, power, and endurance—playing to his strengths. Lucy, on the other hand, tried to use variations of shots to catch Ron off balance. Taking control of the net and making important drops from far back, she made Ron work for every point.

Another sharp blast from Lucas's whistle signalled the end of practice and time to go home. As the guys all were changing from their gym clothes, everyone was thinking of Ron's safety and the possibility of a stalker hounding him. But they didn't want to bring it up and unnecessarily scare him when he needed to feel safe. The eerie silence was broken by Xu, who addressed the elephant in the room.

"Ron, if you want, I can ask my parents to escort your vehicle back home. It's not a bother, and it would be safer for you."

"Thanks, Xu, but I think I'll be alright. If some madwoman comes after me, I'll be sure to put up a good fight." Holding his arms up like a boxer, Ron made some imaginary jabs at his invisible adversary.

"Just be careful, Ron. You never know."

Giving a thumbs-up, Ron walked to his car and, after initially being confident in his safety, made a quick look to make sure he didn't see that small car again in the parking lot.

After dressing into his funeral attire in the change room, Ron drove back to Surrey and arrived at the cemetery. He entered the room and sat on a bench, spotting Annie and her kids at the very front. When it was time to pay his last respects, Ron walked up and turned around, offering Annie his condolences for her loss. Patting her hand, he reassured her that everything would be alright as she wiped a tear from her face.

Driving back home was intense to say the least, as every few seconds he checked all his mirrors for that threatening car. Running off adrenaline and with heightened alertness, Ron was relieved to finally arrive home, seeing the familiar door and garage, which promised safety from his vehicular stalker.

As he opened the door, a familiar, delicious smell hit his nose, and he immediately knew Mom was making Maui ribs, or *pie gwat*. The familiar aroma of herbs and spices made Ron's stomach gurgle. His fear of being followed had made him forget how hungry he was.

He walked in to see Mom cooking as usual and Dad reading his economic magazine. "Hey, Mom, hey, Dad. Dinner smells nice!" he said. Then he walked over to the pans and smelled the searing ribs.

Mom smiled, looking at her son's hungry face. "Go wash up, and we'll be done cooking when you come down, alright?"

"Sounds like a deal! Oh, and there's something I need to tell you guys when I get back."

Dad simply looked up and smiled, not the least suspecting that something was awry with his son.

Washing up, Ron tried to scrub away all the fear, insecurity and worry that had built up that day. But no amount of water and scrubbing could erase the sticky, entrapping fear he felt about returning to work the next day.

After finishing washing up, he went to check his emails one more time before getting to dinner. An email from

Annie caught his eye, and he opened it, finding a letter from her:

> Hello Ron,
>
> I appreciate you coming to Garret's funeral, as when I saw you there, I felt like there was light at the end of the tunnel. You are a good friend, Ron, and I hope we'll keep in touch in the near future.
>
> Yours,
>
> Annie

Smiling at her gratitude, Ron hoped he would be able to see her again soon. When he got downstairs, he found that Mom was just finishing up setting up the table.

"Right on time! Your mother was right all along," Dad said. Then he took a five-dollar bill out of his wallet and gave it to Mom with a minor look of resignation on his eyes.

"Why are you paying Mom?" Ron was quite confused. It wasn't like Dad to pay Mother, as they shared all the finances and accounts.

Looking defeated, Dad confessed to Ron. "I bet your mother five dollars that you would come after dinner was fully set. Your mother bet the opposite. I simply can't beat the intuition of your mother, that's for sure!"

"You have no idea, Dad. Every time I plan to do something, Mom always knows what I want to do beforehand. How do you do it, Mom?"

Mother smiled as she gave away her secret. "It's all about knowing your behaviour, habits, and character. I know you and Dad so well, it becomes easy to predict what you both want to do. Sort of like being a detective!"

"Really, dear? Okay, let's try it. What am I about to do right now, honey?" Dad put on the most adorable smile and crossed his arms.

Mom was not the slightest bit unsure. "You're about to pray, dear, before you eat."

Dad's mouth dropped wide open, shocked at how predictable he was. Mom, on the other hand, had a smug "I told you so" look. She laughed at her husband's surprise.

"Mom and Dad, there is something that happened at work today," Ron said. "Someone was stalking me while I drove from work to badminton practice."

Dad instantly had a worried look on his face. "What do you mean 'stalking,' Ron? Like, followed?"

"A small sedan was following me while I drove all the way to Richmond. I was fortunate they got caught at a red light, but I don't know what to do. If I go back to work tomorrow, they might be there again."

Mom likewise was concerned for her son's safety. "Perhaps you should call the authorities? I mean, it's pretty serious and dangerous for you, Ron."

Ron shook his head. "I'll wait one more day. If I see them at work, I'll call the cops."

As the family started eating, there was an eerie silence as each one thought of what might happen the next day and wondered who would want to stalk Ron. The usual good-natured small talk and conversation were drowned out by the deafening silence.

As they finished the dinner and started clearing the table and washing the dishes, Mom took Ron's hand and warned him. "Ron, please be safe, alright? We already lost Daniel. I don't want to lose you as well. Promise me you'll be careful?" Mom was always serious, calm, and composed, but for the first time, Ron saw a frightened look creep across her face.

Ron hugged her, trying to reassure her of his safety. "Of course, I'll be safe, Mom. Don't fret. If worse comes to worst, I'll call the cops, okay?"

"Take care of yourself, Ron," she said. "I know you probably feel you can fight your way out of any trouble, but there are some really bad people out there, people with no mercy or compassion and who are bent on evil."

After rinsing the last dish, Ron gave a soapy hug to his parents and headed off to bed upstairs. Before he went to sleep, he sent an email to Annie, asking if they could meet at a coffee shop:

> Hey Annie,
>
> I'm just wondering if you wanted to meet at Surrey Café so we could talk? There's something I wanted to ask you. So, if you're not busy tomorrow evening, I'd like to have a chat.
>
> Regards,
>
> Ron

Lying down on his bed, he slowly drifted off to sleep, thinking of Annie and her kids rather than the frightening stalker at work. Holding little Denver in his arms in his imagination, Ron rocked the baby to sleep, humming a lullaby Ron learned as a child:

> Little one, going down is the sun,
> Little one, I hope you had fun,
> Little one, you've been trouble; a ton,
> Little one, going down is the sun,
> Little one, who will you dream of, someone?
> Little one, when it's bath time you run,
> Little one, a comfy bed you have won,
> Little one, going down is the sun.

Ron slowly opened his eyes, waking up to the sound of birds chirping. Checking the clock, he saw he had woken on time, so he went about getting ready for work. After washing up, he bounded down the stairs once again and set about getting his breakfast cereal. As he was taking his bowl to the table, Dad took hold of him and looked him straight in the eye, as serious as he could be.

"Ron, remember what you promised your mom, okay? Stay safe. If anything happens, call the cops, and call us as well."

Giving Dad a nod and salute, Ron dove headfirst into his cereal, attacking it with a vengeance. After he finished his breakfast, he said his goodbyes and drove to work, but not without constantly checking the rearview mirror in a paranoid manner, seeing if anyone was following him.

Arriving at work, he scanned the parking lot to see if the suspicious car was parked nearby. Not seeing it anywhere, he grabbed his bag and entered the office, greeting Clyde the guard.

"Hey, Clyde. It's probably nothing, but there was someone following me as I drove from work to Richmond yesterday. I'm not sure who or why, but I just wanted to let you know there might be a stalker around."

"What type of car was it? I'll do a round check of the parking lot to be safe."

"Um, it was a smaller sedan, dark grey, and in old condition. Thanks, Clyde."

Nodding to Ron, Clyde got up to patrol the parking lot, alerted to the possibility of an offender.

Entering the office, Ron punched in and went up to Terry to get his assignments from the second floor. Returning to the first floor, he put away his assignments and went to the break room to get his usual coffee. The workday seemed like any other, with the hum of conversation in the background broken only by the sound of printers and copiers. Suddenly an unfamiliar noise sounded, something like firecrackers.

Pop! Pop! Pop! Pop!

It was accompanied by the sound of screams coming from the front desk and reception area.

Dozens of heads poked up over the cubicle walls as people strained to see what was going on.

Rhonda rushed over to where Ron was, holding her phone as she was trying to call 911. She put a finger to her mouth to signal him to be silent. Quietly telling the authorities where they were and what was happening, she silently mouthed to Ron: "Walter is shooting people."

Ron maneuvered his way across the office to get as close as he could to Walter. He could hear him interrogating a worker in the cubicle next to him.

"Where's Garret?" Walter was asking. "Tell me or I'll kill you!"

"Garret's not here, Please, Walter, Garret's—"

Pang!

Ron could hear the sound of the worker's head thudding onto the floor. Gauging where he thought Walter was going, Ron tried to get in a position behind Walter so he could tackle him from behind.

The sound of sirens told Ron that the authorities had arrived, and pretty soon cops would be coming to save them. Hearing footsteps, Ron realized that Walter was heading towards his desk, where Rhonda was hiding, Ron had to act quickly to stop the shooter.

Ron then heard Rhonda shouting, "Walter! No, leave me alone!"

"Someone better tell me where Ron and Garret are, or I'll kill Rhonda." Walter's voice was threateningly chilling and cold, without any emotion.

Then Ron heard a voice shouting, "Walter Campbell, this is the police! Put down your weapon and put your hands on your head!"

Grabbing Rhonda as a hostage, Walter pointed the gun at

her head, shouting at the top of his lungs: "If any police officers come in, I'll shoot her! I'll kill her!"

Seeing the police officers entering the office and slowly inching forward, Ron could see Walter was running out of options and that he would be forced to kill Rhonda. Wanting to ensure the safest outcome, Ron stood up and alerted Walter to his presence.

"Walter, I'm here. Let Rhonda go."

"No! If I die, she dies too. Ron, this is all your fault, you know. If you hadn't complained to Garret about me, I would've still been working! Because I lost my job, I lost custody of both my kids! You ruined my life, Ron—you and Garret—and I'm going to make you guys pay for it."

Holding up his hands, Ron tried reasoning with the disgruntled employee. "Walter, don't shoot. We can solve this peacefully. Don't shoot, or we will retaliate." A dozen police officers trained their weapons on Walter, watching his every move.

"Shooting me isn't going to get your job back, Walter," Ron said. "It was your own actions that led to your dismissal from work. Look, Walter, I know it seems you've got nothing left to lose. But think of your children. If you shoot either of us, how do you think this will end? Your kids will lose a father forever. It's not too late to do the right thing. It's not important how you start, it's how you finish that counts. Now just let Rhonda go—"

Pang!

Walter aimed his handgun at Ron and shot him once, hitting him in the shoulder. Ron fell to the floor, holding his injury. As Walter aimed to shoot him again, Rhonda pushed back at Walter, and his shot missed. In the chaos, she was able to escape from his grasp. The police, having a clear shot at Walter and wanting to limit casualties, then shot Walter multiple times until he fell forward, his face changing from anger to resignation.

Still clutching his shoulder and shaking his head at Walter, Ron was saddened that it had to end this way.

"Rhonda, are you alright?" Ron asked. "It's over, don't worry."

She stood frozen, looking in fear at Walter's dead body, still processing what had just happened.

Wincing, Ron walked over to her and placed a hand on her shoulder, bringing her back to reality. She started crying, and they hugged each other, glad that it was indeed all over.

As the paramedics took Ron away to a hospital for his gunshot wound, he asked them to call his parents and let them know he was okay.

As soon as Ron's parents got the call, they rushed to the hospital, with Dad driving as fast as he could.

Both Mom and Dad were anxious to see Ron, worried about his injury. But at the same time, they were glad that it was only a minor one.

At Burnaby Green Timbers, Ron was taken to the emergency department, where his shoulder was to be treated. A doctor came to see him, explaining the situation to him after an MRI.

"You're very fortunate, Ron. It seems the bullet just hit the flesh of your arm near your shoulder, so you're looking at a possible full recovery very soon. We'll just stitch you up, and you can probably be released in a few days."

Mom and Dad came shortly after, and Ron hugged Mom while holding Dad's hand as well. Holding back her tears and berating her son and worrying for him at the same time, Mother talked nonstop with her son. "Ron, you promised to keep yourself safe. Thank goodness you're alright. How could you be so reckless? Are you hurt anywhere else?"

"I'm alright, Mom. Don't worry, please. Oh, Dad, could

you phone Annie to tell her I'm in the hospital and that I can't make today's meeting? Her number is on my phone."

Dad nodded. "Sure thing, Ron. Anyone else you want me to phone?"

"No, just Annie for now. Thanks, Dad."

Dad went over to the nurses' station to recover Ron's phone, which had been stored away after he changed into his hospital gown.

He dialed, and when Annie answered, he said, "Yes, Annie, this is Ron's dad. He's in BGT right now. Yes, sure you can video chat with Ron."

After Dad handed the phone over to Ron, Annie expressed her concern for him, but not without a sarcastic punchline to start the conversation.

"Hey, Ron. So you get yourself shot as an excuse to avoid meeting with me?"

Ron smiled at her, playing along with the game. "Oh yes. I was getting cold feet and decided to find an excuse. Getting shot was probably the safest option. Either that or get hit by a car."

Annie laughed. "I'm just glad you're okay, Ron. Thanks for letting me know. Otherwise, I would have wasted quite some time at the café waiting."

Dad took Mom's hand and pulled her away from Ron. "Let's give Ron a bit of room so they can talk, alright, dear?"

Mom nodded in agreement and walked away after stroking Ron's head gently with her hand, just as she had when Ron was a child.

Annie chuckled as she joked around with Ron. "I'd feel sorry for your future wife, having to take care of a baby like you."

Ron was indignant at the harsh judgement, but he still smiled. "I can take care of myself, you know. This mama's boy can drive standard, is a decent cook, has a well-paying job, and is in tip-top shape. Oh, and did I mention I can do my own laundry?"

"Wow, you can do your own laundry?" Annie wasn't the least impressed. "But can you fold your laundry?"

Ron scoffed. "Who needs to fold laundry? You'll just unfold it when you wear it anyways. Waste of time, all that folding."

Getting serious, Annie was concerned about Ron's safety, wondering how he got shot.

"So, what's the story about how you got injured? Did you get robbed?"

"No, no, there was a disgruntled employee at BC Electric who I snitched on, which ended up resulting in him being terminated from his position. Cutting it short, he blamed me and Garret for losing custody of his kids, so he wanted to get revenge on us both."

Annie was shocked but also a bit confused. "So you just let yourself get shot? What if he'd killed you?"

"Well, he was holding a hostage, and I knew the police would shoot him before he could kill me—or that's what I hoped at least, until he shot me first. I tried reasoning and talking him out of it, but he was insistent on getting revenge."

"He didn't know Garret had passed away?" Annie couldn't understand why someone would attack Garret.

"Apparently no. He killed a few colleagues of mine, asking where Garret was. He didn't believe Garret was gone already."

They kept talking for another thirty minutes, sharing compassion for one another; as one was concerned for the other's health, while the other was concerned for the other's loneliness.

When Mom and Dad came back, Annie was just about to

leave the video call, having to care for her two kids back home.

Saying goodbye, Ron gave back the phone and lay down with a silly grin on his face. Mom and Dad, were going to stay the night with Ron, sleeping in the chairs by the bed. Every few hours, a nurse checked up on him, gauging his blood pressure and temperature.

The next morning, he was tucking into the hospital breakfast like no tomorrow, pleasantly surprised at the good quality of the food. There were warm croissants, eggs, and sausage, along with coffee and orange juice.

Dad had gone to the coffee shop downstairs and bought some cheese-and-egg breakfast sandwiches for Mom and Ron. Soon after breakfast, the doctor came by to inform the Lees that Ron was free to go after a final checkup at ten thirty. Ron thanked the doctor for looking after him. Mom and Dad did likewise—grateful for the health care provided.

Ron called Annie and told her that he was being released from the hospital and that he would be going home very soon. He laughed as he heard her kids crying in the background.

"I'm sorry, Annie. Did I call you at a bad time? Sounds like a battle's going on over there." As if on cue, a clanging sounded, verifying a plate had dropped on the floor. This was followed by a frustrated lecturing by Annie.

"Denver, we do not throw food around. Please finish your breakfast. No, that's your milk bottle, don't— Oh my goodness! Sorry, Ron, I'll call you back when this gong show is over, alright?"

"Sounds like you need some help with your terrible two. I'll be home, so call me whenever!"

Mom and Dad both smiled, looking at one another, nodding in agreement. Ron seemed the happiest he had been in a long time—as if he was ready to face the new in his life.

Ron looked at both his parents, hiding his embarrassment at letting them see his affection for Annie and her kids. "You two weren't supposed to be eavesdropping, you know!" Ron started to blush, realizing he had been exposed.

As the nurse came to take his vitals one last time, Ron went through the routine checkup. First, she put a clamp on his finger to read his oxygen levels, then an inflatable bag around his arm to get his blood pressure. Lastly, a thermometer was put under his tongue to check his temperature.

"Everything looks good," the nurse said. "Just go on to the nurses' station to sign some release forms, and you can be discharged from the hospital as soon as you're done with that. It was nice meeting you."

As Ron got up and walked with his parents to the station, many female nurses were smiling at him, admiring his muscular build.

As they walked to the parking lot, Dad and Mom chuckled after whispering to one another. Ron looked at them quizzically, wondering what was so funny.

"Your mom and I noticed that every nurse on the ward was checking you out," Dad said.

Ron's jaw dropped as his face turned into dire horror at the embarrassing fact. "What? Are you serious? I guess my good looks can be a curse sometimes."

Dad smiled mischievously. "If you want to look uglier, I can make you a mask."

Ron simply looked up at Dad and shook his head at his silly suggestion. After finding their car, everyone got in and headed back home after what seemed like two action-packed days.

As they arrived back at the house, there was a sense of relief that everything was going to be okay and that things would be somewhat more normal. Ron wanted to shower, but he recalled the nurses telling him not to get his wound wet. Doing so would make the healing process longer than if it stayed dry.

Dad turned on the TV, and the news reporters were still talking about the shooting at Ron's workplace.

"We are learning more about the horrific shooting at BC Electric yesterday, and we have confirmed that four employees were killed, including the company's security guard. Police have identified the shooter as Walter Campbell, a former employee of BC Electric. Police shot Walter after he shot a fifth employee in the shoulder while holding a hostage. The employee who was shot has been released from hospital, and a vigil will be held for the four workers who passed away. While police have yet to confirm a motive, some witnesses described Campbell as a disgruntled former employee who had been fired for misbehaviour and malicious conduct at work. Several witnesses claimed that he was seeking revenge on the company for terminating his position."

Mom and Ron walked to the TV as well, listening to the chilling details.

"You know, if Walter was the one following me the day before, I might not have survived if he caught me at badminton practice," Ron said.

"Well, Son," Dad said, "the important thing is that you're okay and the shooter is gone. Although it's sad that four of your colleagues were killed."

"Well, it's about time we got some proper food. How does lasagna sound to you boys?" Mom asked.

Just the thought of her pasta made Ron salivate. "That sounds awesome, Mom! Do you want me to help you grate the cheese?"

"Just be careful you don't cut yourself. Your father lost a chunk of his thumb from shredding carrots."

Dad gave them a thumbs-up, showing them the scar from his culinary accident.

"Your mother is extraordinary when it comes to kitchen technique. You know, having been married to her for more than thirty years, I can say that she has injured herself only once that I know of. That's how amazing she is!" Kissing Mom's head, Dad went to feed the fish, which were still in glass jars till Dad could find an aquarium large enough to satisfy his wants.

Ron watched as Mom boiled water for the pasta sheets and started mincing the beef, her strong arms chopping away rhythmically.

"Is that enough cheese, Mom?" Ron asked. "There's about a bowlful here."

Mom walked over and took a look. "Yes, that's good enough, Ron. Thanks for the help. I got it from here. Go check up on your dad."

Ron washed his cheesy hands and went to watch Dad meticulously feeding his fish, making sure every jar got enough food for the hungry fish.

There were three different types of feed: algae disks for bottom feeders, shrimp pellets for catfish, and flakes for the rest of the fish.

Dad observed every fish, making sure each got enough to eat but not so much that they got bloated. He once told Ron that fish are fairly simpleminded. If they see food, they'll eat it even if they're full already. Finally, Dad took some vegetables from the freezer—a carrot slice and cucumber slice—and gave them to the shrimps to pick over. The shrimp ferociously grabbed at the vegetables with their claws and ate so much carrot that their bodies turned orange from the carrot in their stomachs.

Leaving Dad with the fish, Ron went upstairs to check his emails. Several employees had emailed him with good wishes, thanking him for his bravery and hoping that he would get better soon. Scrolling through them, he found one from Annie, sent to him earlier that morning.

Hi Ron!

It was relieving to talk with you and know that you were okay after being shot. When I first heard you were in the hospital, I was worried sick. I was just wondering if you're up for it, do you want to have that coffee together that was postponed by the shooting? You said there was something you wished to talk about?

Yours,

Annie

Ron smiled at the letter, happy he would have the opportunity to talk with Annie.

Hello Annie!

You know what? Coffee sounds amazing to me. Perhaps tomorrow afternoon? See you then!

Ron

CHAPTER 16

NEW BEGINNINGS

Two years after the attack on BC Electric, life was indeed back to normal for the most part. But in some ways, it would forever be changed.

Ron opened his eyes in the morning, waking to the smell of cooking in the kitchen. Yawning as he walked down the stairs, he smiled as he saw Annie cooking breakfast in the kitchen.

"Good morning, dear. Did you get the kids up yet?" she asked. "Ricardo will be late for school if they sleep in any longer."

"I'll get them. Give me a minute. My breath smells like garbage."

After washing up, Ron went over to Denver and Ricardo's room, opened the door, and saw his two step kids sleeping peacefully in their bunk bed. Going over to Ricardo first, he tapped his shoulder, causing him to wake up. But tapping Denver's shoulder didn't wake him up, so Ron simply took his bed cover and yanked it away, exposing him to the cold and waking him up instantly.

"Time to get up, boys. C'mon, wake up. Mom's making breakfast. It'll get cold soon. Here, let's get you down, buddy."

Holding Denver and lifting him from the top bunk to the floor, Ron watched as they both scurried to the washroom to brush their teeth.

As he bounded back downstairs, Annie gave him a "you know better" look, disapproving of the bad example he was setting.

"If our kids learn to run down the stairs as you do, one day they might get hurt," she said.

"Sorry, dear. Slower it is!" True to his word, Ron began moving in extra-slow motion, setting each plate with meticulous detail and minute movements. Annie took one look and just started laughing, unsure what to say to Ron's silly antics.

Both Ricardo and Denver barreled downstairs and took their spots at the table, leaving the head of the table for Ron, while the other end was reserved for Annie.

Before she sat down, Annie spooned scrambled eggs onto everyone's plate, while Ron sternly warned them to wait for her before starting to eat. Next came the hash browns—crispy, fried potato shreds. Lastly, there was toast with two jars of peanut butter to spread by themselves.

As Annie finally sat down, Ron nodded, signalling that the kids could start eating. Ricardo set about pouring ketchup onto his eggs, while Denver waited for Annie to spread his toast with peanut butter. Ron waited for Ricardo to finish with the ketchup. When the child was done, Ron took the bottle and put some on his plate to dip his hash browns in.

"Honey, after work, when we pick up Denver and Ricardo, do you want to visit my parents?" Ron asked. "If you feel too tired, though, we can go next time."

Denver looked up after hearing Ron mention his parents.

"Grandpa and Grandma? Cannae me go? Grandma gives lotsa food."

Annie laughed as she wiped her son's face. "Yes, although I don't think you need more food, Denver. You're chubby enough, my darling!"

Frowning, little Denver sucked in his tummy and his cheeks, trying to look as skinny as possible before giving up and going straight back to eating.

"I'll tell my mom to let off the treats," Ron said, laughing. "How about you, Ricardo? Want to see Grandpa and Grandma?"

"Grandpa always smells like curry, but I like to play foosball with him," the little boy replied.

"Well, dear, it looks like the ball is in your court," Ron said. "Visit or no visit? That is the question."

"Okay, okay let's go," Annie said. "But you'll have to let me ask your mom about your most embarrassing stories. I can't get enough of those," she said with a laugh.

"Honey, you make a hard bargain. Fine, embarrassing stories it is."

Bargaining was also present at work, as Rhonda, the new supervising manager, wanted to trade her Boston cream donut for Ron's jelly-filled donut.

"Aw, c'mon, Ron," she said. "I thought you liked chocolate? Please? Can I have the jelly one?"

Ron promptly took a bite out of the delicious jelly-filled pastry, marking the end of the discussion.

Clearing up his station and giving Rhonda one last pile of papers to review, he punched out and headed to pick up Ricardo at kindergarten while Annie picked up Denver from daycare. Ron missed driving his blue sports car, but he had gotten used to driving the family SUV and didn't mind it as much, even with the sports car being stored in the garage.

After Ron found Ricardo in the school, the two headed

for Grandpa and Grandma's place, which was only a few minutes' drive away. Calling Annie by wireless Bluetooth, Ron reported that they were on the way there.

Pulling into the driveway, Ron looked nostalgically at the familiar place he'd grown up in. Some part of him would always remember the old house as his home.

Opening the car door, he stayed back a bit to soak in all the good things that had come on him of late. Watching little Ricardo scurry over to the doorway and ring the bell, Ron smiled as he watched his parents open the door. His whole family was together; happy, and content—full of laughter, joy, and vitality. They'd withstood failures, sorrows, and pain, weathering the storm of life at its toughest moments. While they weren't immune to disaster, learning to move on and keep trying was indeed a blessing in disguise. The pain eventually healed, and when it did, each one became even stronger than before—growing tough and calloused to misfortune and tragedy. For life does not consist of only good things. It is peppered with spots of sorrow that can hinder moving on. But all in all, it was the many forms of hope held by each one that led to their own, uniquely fulfilled life—something that was made possible by simply not giving up.

As he shut the car door behind him, Ron suddenly found himself in some sort of hospice, restrained in a mobile bed. Cramming his eyes shut and shaking his head in fright, he zoned back into his reality and followed Ricardo as he entered his home.

Then he closed the door to keep out the frightening vision in his mind, thinking nothing of it and getting back to enjoying his renewed family life.

Manufactured by Amazon.ca
Bolton, ON

27208853R00136